Fixing Nigeria

CHUKS EMMANUEL INYABA-NWAZOJIE

Copyright © 2016 Chuks Emmauel Inyaba-Nwazojie
All rights reserved
First Edition

PAGE PUBLISHING, INC.
New York, NY

First originally published by Page Publishing, Inc. 2016

ISBN 978-1-68348-847-7 (Paperback)
ISBN 978-1-68348-848-4 (Digital)

Printed in the United States of America

Dedication

To the memory of Dad, Udorah and Mon, Eziamaka, I can't find a enough word to adequately thank you for everything you have done from your unconditional love to raising me in a stable household where you instilled in me traditional values and thought all your children to celebrate and embrace life. I am blessed to have you as my parents and role-models. And to Sunday, Francis, Mary rose, Obiageli, Ngozi, Helen, Anthonia, Fidelia, and Ijeoma thanks for all the wonderful memories of growing up, as well as your unconditional support and encouragement. Not forgotten is my two younger brothers, Cyril and Augustine may their memory live forever. And to the Nigerian masses who despite the economic hardships kept hope alive. The best is yet to come! It is my desire that this book reaches your hands and inspires you to love your country more and stand up and fight for your rights. For all my wonderful friends both old and new thanks for always being there for me.

Finally, this dedication cannot be complete without giving thanks to almighty God who gave us knowledge, understanding and wisdoms to do great things for one another. I thank the Lord who inspired the writing of this book.

Our lives begin to end the day we become silent about things that matters, Life's most persistent and urgent question is, what are you doing for others? Martin Luther King, Jr

Acknowledgments

To my wife Akuchi Mary rose Inyaba

Thank you for life of an abundance love. I thank you for supporting me every step of the way both in thick and torn. Thank you for being the best champion anyone could ever ask for. I love you.

To my brother John& Francis Inyaba

I watched you through childhood to adulthood you have always reminded me the meaning of having good brothers. I have always counted on you to run an errand for me and you have never disappointed. Thank you for being the greatest brothers I could have. I love you more than any word can express. I know you are waiting to read this book.

To my sisters Obiageli&Ngozi

Thank you for always caring. Thank you for your love and your continuous support. Thank you for the appetizing and delicious dishes you always cook for me. I love you.

To Helen& Uche

Thank you for saving my life the day a doctor diagnosed me as a malaria patient and gave me malaria injection instead of treating me as a diabetes patient. My blood sugar was shooting up to 850 to 1000 and I was passing out but miraculously God sent you to visit the house from a far distance. When you saw my condition you forgot your family and refused to abandon me. You and Uche mounted a night vigil and prayed for me for more eighteen hours until in the morning when I was rushed to the hospital. I will never forgot. You were my angels. My sister who bath and fed me with spoon like a baby thank you. My friend who paid the hospital bill thank you. I love you all.

Last but the least to the guy who inspired this book and to Nigerians I love you more than words can express. I can't wait to see your dreams of a better and a great country come through. The best is yet to come? I love you all

"Reforms, reforms, reforms, reforms, reforms, and reforms!" is an absolute answer to the Nigerian problems. The status quo should be ended. End the status quo now!

Uproot, destroy, and rebuild. Rebuild better, bigger, and stronger (Jeremiah 1–10).

A gentleman stopped me on the night of Dec. 30, 2013, at Ojelegba Road, Surulere, Lagos, Nigeria, when I was walking back home and said to me, "Sir, my name is ――――. I am coming from the church service. Nigerian churches all over the nation have begun twenty-one days and nights of fasting to pray for Nigeria. The masses are praying to God to grant them a visionary and articulate leaders who can solve the problems in the nation." He said that the masses are suffering, and they want an answer and a change in the nation.

He continued, "Sir, I graduated from the university ten years ago, but I have never found a real job. I am a petty trader because there is no job. It is difficult to make ends meet. Many Nigerian youths are fleeing the country on a daily basis in search of greener pastures overseas and to escape poverty and unemployment.

"Many graduates I have known since my school days are still seeking for job many years after their graduation. They are stocked in the job market without hope of finding a job. The people are suffering, except the 1 percent Nigerians who are holding the oil wealth. These are some of the reasons why Nigerians are flocking to the church to pray and fast for the next twenty days and nights for God's mercy on the country and the masses. Nigerians are tired, and they have exhausted their patience and energy waiting for the Messiah to come. We need help."

He told me that the reason he stopped me was because he saw me as a gentleman and an approachable person who seems to look like someone who is suited enough to answer some of these burning issues facing our country.

I said to him, "Are you a journalist?"

"No, sir," he said.

"What is your question?" I asked him.

He then said to me, "Sir, what do you think about the problems facing Nigeria?"

I answered him by telling him that the problems in Nigeria were created by former civilians and military leaders that began a day after gaining independence from Great Britain.

I told him that tribalism, bribery, corruption, and fraud took root a day after the nation was granted independence from Great Britain in 1960. Because Nigerian politicians allowed tribalism, bribery, fraud, and corruption to take center stage in every public policy they enacted, the nation was unable to function effectively, hence serious national problems developed and went unchecked for years.

Because of the failure of our political leaders, the military boys hijacked the government and created the greatest problems for the nation that remain unsolved till today. Nigeria is a cancerous nation that can be cured if Nigerians themselves can take action to reclaim their country from the politicians and former failed military leaders who are still menacing and intruding in the affairs of this nation.

He asked, "Sir, how will this happen?"

I told him that God has been so kind and nice to the nation when he blessed them with abundance of natural resources, which includes oil, a gift of intelligent people, and a beautiful country, but all lay wasted due to tribalism, bribery, corruption, nepotism, and mismanagement. I further let him understand that the masses have the power to determine how they want their nation to be ruled by using their democratic voices and power to choose wisely those they want to rule them. They also have the right to fire the nation's polluters. He asked me, "Sir, what do you think is the solution?" I gave him an answer, but the answer should be a last-resort action should every other solution fails; it will be revealed towards the end of this paper. However, the causes and solutions to Nigerian problems will be discussed throughout this paper, which will be in the form of government reforms.

Let me just say this to the Nigerian masses who have fasted for their country for twenty-one days and nights, your prayers have been answered.

God's message to you is uproot, destroy, and rebuild, and rebuild bigger, better, and stronger. The hour has come for change and to pave the way for a new nation for all Nigerians. I was visiting from New York, New York, USA (2013–2014).

Before I start, I would like to make one declaration, and that is Nigeria is a united country except when the Nigerian politicians use various racial and ethnic categories to divide and conquer the Nigerian population. Because of this, the federal government became the greatest promoter of tribalism, favoritism, nepotism, and corruption, using these to create the biggest government enterprises that benefit only the ruling political class, families, friends, and cronies while the masses bite the nails.

Introduction

This paper is based on what I have observed unfolding in Nigeria from October 1, 1960, to the present time. What I have witnessed as a kid, a youth, and adult, I have seen the good, the ugly, and the ugliest.

It may be because of my interest and passion for this nation that made me to continue to watch and monitor its progress and failures over the years in which I want to reveal the result of this effort. My research came from my personal experiences, facts, eyewitnesses' stories, person-to-person interviews and phone call interviews, imagination, and observations.

The primary purpose of this paper is to discuss and analyze the genesis of Nigerian trolley problem based on my perspective as a citizen. The goal is to tell the truth, noting but the truth, regarding how one of the world's biggest oil-producing nations remain a poor country. Judging from my investigations, the solution to the national problems would be reforms, reforms, and nothing but reforms, which will be discussed throughout this paper.

One persistent question that can always be ask is why the politician and the former military leaers miss governed this nation called Nigeria?

Neither the politicians nor the former military leaders has been able to tell the nation the whereabouts of billions and billions of dollars earned from oil. Nigerians are still waiting fir answer. They deliberately and purposeful uprooted and destroyed every critical infrastructure left behind by the colonial masters, drove out international investors, and seized their businesses and handed them over to rogue Nigerians who were incapable of running these businesses, leading to massive economic, political, and social collapse of the nation. Their actions created the greatest sufferings for the masses. They blinded the people with ignorance of about what the government does with the nation's oil wealth.

A once progressive, forward-looking nation was allowed to fall flat on its face because it has been run by rogue leaders. Their actions and deeds broke the nation into pieces, and for years they failed to fix the nation they have broken, leading to untold sufferings for the masses.

This paper will try to detail the real problems with Nigeria and show the way and manner to fix it with reforms. The nation's leaders run the biggest government enterprises that benefit only the few in the country.

It has been more than half a century of government failures in this country, which now needs to be addressed. This paper tends to disclose the names of those who created these problems for the nation.

Being a Nigeria, I considered a duty to write in black and white the little things I know about the country. This paper will discuss in full detail how the country can once again become the African nations' powerful economic nation, how to rebuild the nation and create jobs for the people so that they can go back to work and start to rebuild their wasted lives again, how to give them the opportunity to rebuild a better progressive nation and stronger society.

The goal and purpose of this paper is to contribute positively about how the nation can begin to lay a solid foundation on a solid rock for a better Nigeria. My greatest dream is to see this nation become the most progressive economy in Africa and around the world that will create a better life for its people and everyone that call the nation his or home regardless of color. It will be a new nation that will create a social welfare to help those in need.

No one would have suggested that Nigerian leaders in particular and African leaders in general will employ the use of "defense mechanism" to deny their failures. They turn around to blame colonialism even though they are the new colonialists who are colonizing their own people when they steal and pocket their nation's collective wealth.

However, they wouldn't remember to employ the Maslow's hierarchy of needs, which stated that our basic needs start from the bottom to the top. Instead, once they wrestled power from the people, they will start from the top and will never able to reach the bottom because by the time they finish enjoying themselves at the top and when they try to climb down to the bottom, the ladder might have fallen down; therefore, no one else goes up to the top of the ladder. Because of their actions and deeds, they kept the nation and the people backwards and in darkness.

They didn't know how to create the greatest happiness for the greatest number of people, but they, however, know how to create the greatest happiness for the few people who somehow believe they own the country, which enabled them to rip off their country. These are some of the biggest problems facing the country that require an immediate fixing. That is what this paper is set out to do

I have identified a number of areas to be reformed and fixed. The entire nation is begging for a complete makeover. Every operating area in the nation should be on the table to face reforms. During the reforms the future of generation and generations of Nigerians to come should be at the back of our mind.

Nigeria and African World Economic Forums

Even though now their new defense mechanism has become the use of neocolonialism to deny their failures while at the same time staging Nigerian-world economic forum or African-world economic forums because it gives them another opportunity to spend billions of dollars to stage these forums for the purpose of enriching themselves and families and not help their nation to achieve any meaningful economic development.

The so-called economic forums are just mere cosmetics that lack substance because it will never convince international investors to start rushing to Nigeria or any other African nation to invest with seeing reforms. Nigeria and African leaders must understand that without reasonable reforms, no honest international business investors will bet their money in these nations. Reforms must first take place because these nations' economic system is broken.

Nigerian leaders cannot solve its problems without first initiating top-to-bottom reforms because the nation is a "failed state" that should start all over again and fix a broken nation before anything else could take place. They should stop pretending and start to be serious on ways to fix the nation.

If Nigeria and the less of African nations refuse to reforms to fix their broken nations, no amount of economic forums will help them to restore their nation economically. Their quest for economic growth will remain a tall dream because the same rogue leaders will remain in power, and bribery and corruption will never be dealt with, and the people will continue to suffer. The nation will remain a failed state.

In this paper I talk about the African continent as a whole because all the African nations have similar problems as Nigeria.

Also, no amount of African world economic forum will be beneficial to African nations until each and every one of them agree to first reform their nations' failed economic system. Nigerian leaders in particular and African leaders in general are always looking for dubious ways to steal and squander their nation's wealth by falsely using the name of holding economic forum after economic forum that never get these nations anywhere because they have refused reforms. Because of this reason, it will be difficult for them to attract the best and honest investors to their countries.

Have Nigerian leaders and the less of African leaders forgotten how they seized, uprooted, and destroyed international investments in their countries and threw out European investors from their countries from 1948 to the 1980s?

At that time, each and every newly independent African nation did the same, except South Africa because of Nelson Mandela. These are some of the reasons African nations become known as failed states.

I did not set out to write this paper for any other reason other than that I love this country and the people, but I have witnessed the faces of the suffering that is not supposed to exist in an oil-rich country. That is what troubles the Nigerian masses and perhaps the international community. Those who hold power use their fellow citizens as a doormat.

I am not writing because I know too much but because I believe my opinion of what I know as a citizen will help to stimulate national and international debates about how to fix leadership's failures in Nigeria in particular and Africa in general.

I have no other ambition rather than to write so that someone can stand up and take the responsibility to fix a broken nation.

I believe in the word of JFK of the United States, who told his nation, "Ask not what your country can do for you, but ask what you can do for your country."

I believe in Martin Luther King Jr., who rejected unjust and immoral laws and inequality and fought with his life for the civil rights to be passed and signed into law by President Johnson for every American.

I believe in Fredrick Douglas, a former slave who taught himself how to read and write despite the obstacles in front of him. He succeeded and used his knowledge to fight for the freedom of his fellow slaves still in captivity.

I believe In Nelson Mandela, who accepted to go to prison for the sake of his people and nation. He was jailed for twenty-seven years, and when he was freed, he forgave his tormentors and embraced peace and a "rainbow nation" and initiated reconciliation with all South Africans no matter what color they were.

They all paid a big price for the sake of their people and nations so that they will be peace, unity, and equality in the world.

Their work and effort must never be allowed to fade.

I also believe in my father, Udorah Francis Inyaba, a palm wine tapper, who said to me, "Son, whatever you do in life, never forget the poor, and if you climb up the ladder, never pull it down. Leave it for someone else to also climb."

I grew up poor, and that made me understand the ugly part of poverty.

I had wanted to write this paper for years, but I was hoping that things will get better and conditions will improve, but every day in this country the conditions of the people go from bad to worse and graduate to even worst; hence I decided to take action to write this paper because I believe I have received a call that this paper can no longer be postponed. The night of December 30, 2013, stroke my spiritual sensibility to answer a divine call to write this paper now in order to address the biggest issues facing a once great country formerly respected around the world, now becoming a laughingstock around the world.

My name is Chukwujiekwu Emmauel Inyaba-Nwazojie (Chuks). I was born and raised in Nigeria in the former eastern region of the country. I was born in Abatete in Umuebo Village, Abaja. I was born to a father and mother named Francis Udorah and Ezimaka Inyaba. I am a Nigerian-American citizen. I am a businessman, a manager of Seven Stars Import and Export, New York, New York. I studied at Berkeley College, New York, where I earned Associate degree in Applied Sciences 2015.

Even before I dreamt of coming to America, I have seen this nation unfold in many different forms and fashions, which sometimes fascinated me and other times troubles me. I was a kid on October 1, 1960, when the colonial masters granted Nigeria independence. There was joy in all parts of the nation.

My only fun memory was seeing the grown-ups dancing, rejoicing. Schoolchildren were given cows to slaughter to celebrate the much-anticipated freedom.

The politicians and well-heeled Nigerians were uncorking champagne and were drinking the finest imported beers and were having a good bite on the best foods. I guessed life was so good for them. Though many Nigerians still go to bed on empty stomachs, the communities were tight and united.

Early Sixties

My only knowledge of the sixties' political icons like Zik, Awo, Abubakar, Akintola, Ahamed Bello, Mbadiwe, Mike Okpara, R. B. K. Okafor were from cartoons because I couldn't read then. Due to the ways they were cartooned, I often thought they were some kind of space aliens or spirits that touch the ground once in a while and left to come back. Sometimes I saw them as superhumans or untouchables, and the cartoons often scare me as well.

After the Independence Euphoria, October 1, 1960

To us kids, that period marked the end of British rule, and Nigerians were entrusted with their future destiny and the reign of power and its administration and management. Every news we heard was either by word of mouth or by looking at cartoons. To the kids, it was like a fairy tale. We were happy but confused. The politicians rode in big cars, dressed flamboyantly with the most expensive material in the market, swam in ostentatious living with reckless abandon.

Surprisingly, nobody ever thought that the newly independent nation would quickly be divided with tribalism, an introduction of bribery and corruptions by the Nigerian politicians, which began to take shape immediately, not even allowing the independence signature to dry. It was followed with political infighting organized under tribal patronage.

Western Nigerian Political Riots 1965

Western Nigeria exploded into local and national political flames and began to burn. Human beings were roasted alive like chickens day in and day out. Akintola, the then premier of Western Nigeria, and Awolowo, the national opposition leader, fought to the bitter end. Akintola was killed, and Awolowo was tried for treason and sent to jail. The riot in Western Nigeria was nicknamed Operation Wettee because innocent citizens were burned and roasted alive for sake of two political leaders.

The much-anticipated freedom has become nightmarish for the citizens. Abubakar, the then prime minister of Nigeria, I believe, was helpless about how to deal with the Western crisis, and the people of the West burned and roasted each other to death. The only action taken by the federal government was to form the antiriot police named Nigerian Mobile Police to quell the crisis in the West. It was the military coup that brought the crisis to an end.

January 15, 1966, was the day the nation's problems began a journey of no return.

By 1966, it was evidently clear that the politicians had failed. It has reached to the point of no return. Think about it: it was barely six years after independence when the ink was yet dried. Nigeria has gotten a big problem that ended in a short duration of the first republic.

Army

Little did Nigerians know that some young military officers were quite displeased with the politicians and decided that the only solution was a military revolution.

Major Patrick Chukwuma Kadund Nzeagwu, the Coup Leader

A young military officer named Major Patrick Chukwuma Kaduna Nzeagwu, with his fellow young military officers, decided that the only way out was to overthrow the government and eliminate all the major political bigwigs in order to save Nigeria.

Here is what the young military major said about Nigeria's trolley problems and the reasons for the military actions:

> "Our enemies' are the profiteers, the swindlers, the men in high and low places that seek bribes and demand 10 percent, those that seek to keep the country divided permantly so that they remain in office as ministers or VIPS, at

least the tribalist, the nepotists, those that make the country look big for nothing before international circles, those that have corrupted our society and put the Nigerians political calander backwards by their words and deeds." [Major P. Nzeagwu [1966]

Ladies and gentlemen, Major Nzeagwu was 100 percent Nigerian. He identified the nation's trolley problem forty-nine years ago, long before anyone else could see it, and he paid with his own life for telling the truth.

What this young man said forty-nine years ago is true yesterday and today, only that it has gotten worst.

Today in Nigeria, a child five years old and up can only understand that the road to success is to be dubious, to be corrupt, or to engage in criminal activities because of the lack of jobs and because other decent ways of making an honest living are blocked nor are there other opportunities available.

It is a fact that Nigerian people do not have a choice because the system has been structured to function with flagrant disregard of ethics and morals by our political leaders. The system ground rule is, "If you can't beat them, join them." Bribery and corruption are a merry-go-round in Nigeria. It is an invasive cancer that began a day after independence and continues on to this day.

Should Nigeria's past and current leaders happen to lay their hands on this book and read the wisdom of Major Nzeagwu, a young military officer who was just twenty-eight years old when he told Nigerians the undebatable truth about their problems, which the nation's politicians and military leaders ignored for years, I think that these men and women would be ashamed of themselves and the country for their failure to lead.

To Nigerians, your voices are your nuclear bombs. They are your weapons of mass destruction. They are your arms and ammunitions. They are your civil rights They are your liberty. The Nigerian citizens can no longer accept the honor of being second-class citizens in their own country. For years these men and women have run the country with antiquated laws and military orders. It is no longer acceptable to the people. Nigerians, you deserve better.

Major Nzeagwu's coup failure was not his fault, rather the fault of his colleagues, who failed to execute their own part of the assignment, which could be attributed to the corrupt Nigerian system.

As much as I do not support the taking of any life at all, we cannot predict what the military can do because they kill with their guns. Everyone in the country would have preferred that all the politicians marked down during the coup for elimination had the same fate as those of Major Nzeagwu's victim in the North. Perhaps Nigeria would not have fought a civil war. What happened in 1966 was not a cause for any type of celebration. As a nation, no lesson has been learnt forty-nine years after a twenty-eight-year-young military officer identified and alerted the nation about the cause of its trolley problems.

Nigerian politicians since after the civil war ended continued to make the same mistakes that took the nation to a three-year civil war. The same mistakes are repeated over and over and over and over again and again and are getting worse and worse on a daily basis.

According to Nelson Mandela, "A man can have experience and knowledge, but only God can make a man wise." Nigerians are looking to God's anointed wise men and women to lead them to the promised land.

Finally, Major Nzeagwu Patrick Kaduna Chukwuma is my hero and should be the hero of every Nigerian, not because he killed one of the most highly valued Nigerian politicians of our time (that couldn't have happened), but because Patrick had the courage to tell

Nigerians the naked truth about the cause of the nation's problems. That one single truth about Nigeria remains the same yesterday and today but is worse than forty-nine years ago when the statement was made.

Honoring Major Patrick Nzeagwu

It is time Nigerians bury the hatchet and respect and honor the name of this true Nigerian patriot who told the truth about the health of the nation in 1966. To honor him, a Chair of Major Patrick Chukwuma Kaduna Nzeagwu Ethics and Moral Studies Department or Psychology Department should be set in every Nigerian institution of higher learning. It should be made mandatory for every student to study this course before graduating. In addition to this, the Delta State University can be renamed Major Patrick Chuwuma Kaduna Nzeagwu University to honor him. It is very important to return this country back to decency, integrity, honesty, and truth. We want to see a nation where talents, skills, creativity, efficiency, productivity, and predictability will be the nation's motto instead of bribery and corruption taking the upper hand. Decency, honesty, and integrity are required to fight, corruptions, bribery, tribalism, nepotism and favoritisms must be tackled head on if this country want be great. I urge the government, nonprofit organizations, and individuals to make contributions both in kind and cash to honor the name of this true Nigerian patriot. It is important that this scholarly department become a reality in his name.

The Countercoup in 1966

The purpose of this discourse is not to tell the history of the Nigerian Civil War. To the best knowledge of every Nigerian, when the war ended, Nigerians forgave one another and became once again one people and one nation.

The head of state, General Jakub Gowon, declared no winner and no vanquished. But Nigerians cannot honestly discuss their current political, economic, and social predicaments without referencing the war because that was where it all began.

The most painful part of the events that led to the civil war will be omitted here. It is hoped that the nation had learnt its lesson. Never will it happen again.

General Aguiyi-Ironsi, Military Head of State, 1966

One morning, Nigerians woke up to the news that the head of state, General Aguiyi Ironsi, and his host, Colonel Fauyi, the military governor of the western region, had been killed while he was paying a state visit to that region in an attempt to initiate reconciliation among Nigerians due to the first failed coup.

General Ironsi was the first military general of the Nigerian army, a gallant of gallants of soldiers, fine, honest, gentleman soldier. His host, Colonel Fauyi, was also a fine and honest soldier who gallantly fought with his last breath to save his guest but failed and also was butchered in military ways.

Major General Aguiyi-Ironsi, who was the first Nigerian military general and the first military head of state, has not been properly honored by Nigerians and the government.

His name should also be on the Nigerian currency. The military defense academy in Kaduna should be named after him The Abuja

International Airport should be renamed Aguiyi-Ironsi International Airport (AIIA). He truly deserves these honors.

Colonel Fauyi also should be honored as well, and a street name in Abuja Capital should be named after him. These two gallant military officers were true Nigerian patriots who loved their country and wanted to make it better but ended up paying with their lives.

General Aguiyi-Ironsi was butchered, tied to a military jeep, and dragged around the city of Ibadan by his junior military officers.

Colonel Yakubu Gowon, Military Head of State, 1966–1975

There is no amount of excuses can be given for the senseless murder of General Aguiyi Ironsi and Colonel Fauyi other than a revenge killing by the Northern military officers. The lives of another two fine military officers had been taken due to their effort to bring peace and unity to the country. Nigerians can no longer make sense of military officers killing each other for the sake of Political powers they are not train for. When the news came that another young military officer had been chosen to replace the murdered head of state, the nation, though still in mourning, had no choice but to accept the new head of state, an agile, handsome, peaceful-looking military officer who looked fit. Upon accepting the office of the head of state, he appealed for calm with the promise that things will be better. He did try his best. Tensions were high; the action center was in Northern Nigeria.

In the East, Colonel Ojukwu was the military governor, and he was another handsome, gallant young officer. Both men were faced with the toughest decisions to be made: to be one nation, one people or not. They were faced with the toughest decisions of a lifetime. Both men were relatively very young, and they were entrusted with the responsibility of deciding the fate of the nation.

The agonies suffered by one side of the nation caused by another side of the nation were indeed too much to bear. The problems of the nation had become an earthquake waiting to erupt on the nation if no common ground was found; the problem had reached a crossroad. Colonel Ojukwu in the eastern region of the nation had a duty to protect his constituents. On the side of the nation, Gowon as a head of state had a duty to try to keep Nigeria one.

Ojukwu especially was left without any other choice, in view of the events that led to the civil war. Indeed, before the first coup, we rarely saw the army on the street.

When we began to see the faces of these officers for the first time, for example, like Gowon, Ojukwu, and Nzeagwu, it inspired some sense of pride in the nation, leading many young Nigerian men to choose the army as a career. The army was closely united as one Nigeria until the politicians' actions divided the military into tribal lines in the history of Nigeria.

The Nigerian army is one of best legacies that the British colonial masters had left behind. The army was awesome! The Nigerian army should not be blamed for what happened in Nigeria in the sixties. Rather, the whole blame must go to the politicians who failed to do the job they were elected to do.

What is happening in Nigeria today shows that the current politicians have not learnt any lessons from the past. This is part of the urgent reasons why Nigerians should consider a change of power in the nation.

All effort made by both sides not to go to war failed woefully, but Nigerians can always defer to General Gowon. He is a good man, good soldier, and good Christian. The decision to go to war or not go to war was made at the Supreme Military Council level, where he was the chairman and a lone voice Even when he agreed with the Aburi Accord in Ghana, where he reached a peace agreement with Ojukwu that war should be avoided at all costs. They agreed that Biafra can leave the union, but it was not honored by the Nigerian government, hence the start of the civil war in 1967.

Colonel Ojukwu was completely boxed into a corner, and there was no escape route for him. The information coming out from the Nigerian side of nation regarding the fate of Ojukwu's constituents (the Igbos) were terrible, horrible, inhuman, and cannot be printed. Because of all these pains and sufferings and defeats, his constituents amassed on the streets in every town, city, and village, demonstrating against Colonel Gowon's government and urging Colonel Ojukwu to declare war. However, Ojukwu and Gowon continued the effort to find common ground for peace, but the situation continued to deteriorate hour by hour and day by day, hence no agreement was reached to end the drumbeat of an impending war. The provocations on both sides of the divide were so much that no side was ready to reconciliate with the other. General Ojukwu had no choice but to declare the Republic of Biafra because the Igbos has been pushed out from every other parts of the country and were facing genocide.

The Civil War 1967–1970 and My School

In 1967, Nigeria declared war against Biafra, which lasted for three years. Then I was a class 1 student at St. Patrick Secondary School at Oboleke, Nsukka, Nigeria. Nsukka in Eastern Nigeria which shares a common boundary with Northern Nigeria.

All of a sudden I became mysteriously ill, which my school clinic was unable to treat, so they referred me to Park Lane Hospital in Enugu to see the doctor. The trip to the hospital was about 170 to 200 miles, but nonetheless, I must go or die.

As soon as I stepped into the hospital, I felt completely normal to my greatest surprise. To avoid any doubt, I decided that I will consult the doctor. So I went to see the nurse, who issued me a card to see the doctor. When I saw the doctor, he told me after examining me that I was completely normal and that there was nothing wrong with me and that I should go back to school.

My school fell in the hand of the federal forces at the beginning of the war which made it hard for me to go back. As I was set to go back to school, I received a very sad news that the Nigerian Civil War had begun and that the Nigerian military forces had entered and had captured and run over my school and that many students were killed and many escaped.

The Nigerian army entered the school in the dead of the night when students were sleeping. That was the last time I saw my school and my fellow students and classmates. My school and its students became the first casualty of the Nigerian Civil War.

End of Civil War, 1970

In 1970, the Nigeria-Biafra war ended. General Gowon declared no winner and no vanquished. He was a good man.

The Biafra head of state and the commander in chief of the Biafra armed forces, General Ojukwu, had gone outside the country in search of peace but never made it back before the war ended.

Soon, Nigerians of all languages and tribes forgave one another. In fact, they were a bunch of Nigerians who displayed unforgettable kindness by safekeeping the abandoned properties and belongings of their fellow brothers and sisters who crossed over to the other side of the war theater.

There were some others who regarded such properties and belongings as abandoned and seized them as their own. In the end, Nigerians became strongly united.

No more wars! Let's us rebuild our country together to be bigger, better, and stronger for generations and generations of Nigerians to come.

The Economy under Gowon Watch

No doubt General Gowon remains the best president Nigerian people ever had. He is a man of integrity, a gentleman, decent, honest, and was beyond corruption. The economy was so good in his time that Nigerians were living like Europeans during that period of his administration.

He understood that the colonial masters had left behind tangible critical infrastructures to propel Nigeria's economy on to greater heights and prosperity. He expanded the economy in every nook and corner of the country. Foreign investors flocked to Nigeria to invest.

There were jobs, jobs, and jobs! High school graduates had jobs; university graduates had jobs. The private sector was booming; business investment was high.

The middle class flourished. Our cities and towns functioned for twenty-four hours a day, seven days a week. Nigerians were admired and respected around the world. Nigerians lived happily. Bribery and corruption were not yet widespread because Nigerians were contented with what they had then.

Nigerians bought and drove new cars and not used ones. The nation was a magnet for international investors and tourists. His legacies remain but are not functioning well.

After the civil war ended, General Gowon gave twenty British pounds to Igbos.

However, two major mistakes occurred in General Gowon's administration. First mistake was the order that the Igbos coming out of the war should be given only twenty British pounds sterling per person regardless of how much they saved in the bank before the civil war. In fact, before the civil war, the Igbos were the richest Nigerians and had saved billions of British pounds sterling in the bank all over the country, which were abandoned when they fled to Biafra because of the unrest engulfing the nation then.

The order was a gross injustice and inhuman against some citizens of the same nation because the other section of the nation won the war but declared no winner, no vanquished but turned around to loot their wealth.

The Igbos' billions of British pounds sterling were hijacked and seized by the federal government of Nigeria as a punishment for the war. When the war ended, Gowon declared no winner and no vanquished. Why did he allow this to happen? Before the civil war, the Igbos had amassed wealth of millions and billions of British pounds sterling and saved in banks all over Nigeria before fleeing to the eastern region for their safety.

It is time the Nigerian government told the people the true story behind the unjust seizure of this money. They should tell Nigerians exactly how much money was involved and what happened to the money.

How much interest rate payment has this money accumulated over the years since it has been seized? The next step is to tell the Igbos how the federal government plans to return the money back to them.

Return Seized Money to the Igbos

The only way the federal government could return this money is to pay every Igbo family and other non-Igbos affected about forty million naira each to correct this injustice. It is also a good thing that Gowon is still around to tell Nigerians why he allowed this injustice to happen after he declared no winner and no vanquished. The Igbos are entitled to seek justice in the court of law if the federal government fails to return their money. Forty million naira should be paid to every Igbo family by the federal government of Nigeria.

The federal government should set up a board of inquiries to allow Gowon and other living members of the Supreme Military Council to testify and tell the country why the decision was made to treat the Igbos like trash after the war ended. The federal government can as well release the white papers on this matter for all Nigerians and the world to learn about the truth behind the seizure.

Gowon's Second Mistake: The Indigenization Decree

The next mistake was the indigenization decree that uprooted and destructed all the critical infrastructures left behind by the colonial masters and then expelled all international businessmen and businesswomen out of the country, which helped to cripple the Nigerian economy and social lives as well as destructed businesses and jobs in the nation that became the genesis of Nigerian trolley problems. This economic decree badly hurt the nation's economic progress and the people for years, and they have not stopped hurting.

An intelligent elementary school student should have known that the idea to uproot and destroy businesses uprooted in such a manner without a replacement was a bad economic prescriptions and social lyching of the people's way of life.

The nation was visibly unprepared and was just coming out of war. Awolowo, then the finance minister, was the architect of both military decrees of giving twenty British pounds to the Igbos because Gowon and other members of the Supreme Military Council are soldiers who trusted Awolowo, as an elder statesman, to offer good and sound economic advice on the best way to expand the nation's economy. But that advice turned out to be something that ended the nation's advancing progressive economy, which, as a result, put the nation's economic future in tatters and dilemma. On to the present time, nothing has changed.

The idea of the indigenization decree was dubious from start to finish because the country has not laid a claim to any other means of creating jobs or any plan to create other opportunities both direct and indirect ones to grow the economy after seizing, expelling, and selling off these foreign businesses to some few privileged Nigerians, who had no means to run these businesses on their own.

The government knew that no Nigerian owned the intellectual properties or had the money, ability, and management skills to run any of these megacorporations, many of them Fortune 500 companies, yet they blindly proceeded to indigenize them, and the people paid the biggest price for the government's melancholy act. Whether sentiment and tribalism played some roles in making this deadly decision, no one knows, but it is only the authors of the decrees who can tell. The policy was a kind of economic suicide committed against the nation by few privileged Nigerians.

The Overthrow of General Gowon in 1975

It was a year Nigerians will never forget and wish that the military coup of General Mohammed and General Obasanjo never happened. The year 1975 remains the greatest year of nightmare for Nigerians, an experience they would like to forget but cannot.

It was the year that General Murtala Mohammed and his military gangs overthrew the legitimate government of General Gowon on the basis or excuse that Gowon planned to run for president under a political party. Gowon would have been elected as president quite easily if he was not overthrown.

Many Nigerians who thought that Gowon deserved the right to join any political party of his choice were very surprised when he was shoved aside. Nigerians mourned for the nation after the overthrow of Gowon, which became again part of the nation's dark history.

He was a good leader, a decent honest man, a young military officer who fought the war to unite Nigeria. His overthrow was the darkest hour and the darkest day in the history of the nation. He was a true statesman.

General M. Mohammed, Head of State, 1975

After receiving the sad news of yet another coup, Nigerians were quite apprehensive of General Mohammed and his gang of army officers.

However, soon after they knew him very well, he became dear to the people's hearts. This was also because of a story that was told about how he confessed and returned the money he looted from a bank during the war. Because of this single act of boldness and honesty, he instantly became a hero to many Nigerians.

I wish other Nigerians could act in similar a manner, to return their loot and confess, because of the example this man had set on how to be a good citizen and a statesman.

Nigerians expected him to be a good president with high hopes for a better Nigeria, but soon another tragedy befell Nigerians yet again. Just six months into his presidency, it was yet another senseless coup and another senseless murder of the nation's military commander and head of state. It was a really sad day in Nigeria. Nigerians mourned him greatly because they loved him. He was a great soldier and great Nigerian that will forever be remembered.

Brigadier General Obasanjo, the Next Military Head of State, 1976

He was second in command to General Mohammed, so as expected, he was chosen to replace the demised head of state. Because of the love and high expectations Nigerians already had for Mohammed, Nigerians expected his replacement to continue with his good work, so Obasanjo was welcomed with love and open minds. Nigerians assumed he was going to be like Mohammed. Nigerians had placed their bet on Obasanjo that he will be a good leader.

By the time he assumed power, the effects of Awolowo's indigenization policy had become the nation's trolley problem. Nigerians were losing their jobs; businesses were folding up. Once buoyant life enjoyed in the country had become boring, stressful, and nightmarish for the people. Anything seen in view was going out of the windows.

Despite all these, the people had placed the highest expectations on the leadership of General Obasanjo to stop the economic doldrums and jump-start the economy, but instead he chose to go down the same lane of using destructive decrees to further ruin the nation's economy.

Obasanjogate 1976

In his first public policy, he informed the nation about what he called austerity major. His next decree was called the green revolution; that was the first time most Nigerians heard these jargons. Nonetheless, the suffering in the country deepened. Crimes started to rear its ugly head in the nation.

Not satisfied with his first two unworkable economic decrees, Obasanjo once again added one more economic decree he called nationalization of foreign businesses, which was the final deathblow on Nigerian economy that resulted to massive unemployment and business losses.

Combined with Awolowo's indigenization decree, the nation's economy was done forever. It is only reforms that hold the promise to bring Nigerian economy back to life, which no government in Nigeria has attempted.

He became a leader who mindlessly imposed economic sanctions on his own country's economy with military decrees without a foreign nation imposing trade sanctions on the nation. His military decrees brought the nation's economy to destruction for years. He banned importation of goods even though the nation does not produce anything, creating more hardships for the masses.

He introduced a dubious import license for the rich and the higher-up to steal and divert Nigerian oil wealth to their foreign private accounts.

The more and more the Central Bank of Nigeria approved these import licenses for the nation's higher-up, the more Nigerian oil wealth was secretly siphoned into private foreign accounts instead of using it to import the goods it was approved for. At the end, no one else benefitted from this policy except the 1 percent rich Nigerians. The rest suffered nightmares and hardships for untold number of years.

Honestly speaking, no Nigerian supported or liked his military decrees except those few privileged Nigerians who were the beneficiaries. What excuse does he have to bring down a well-established economy causing the uprooting of critical infrastructures left behind by our British masters?

He used the pretense of his green revolution to acquire massive acres of lands at Otta and began his farming project to the surprise of all Nigerians. Even though he was still a military officer and a military head of state, it was an abuse of power and a conflict of interests, but only in Nigeria could this happen.

I guess he received his farming idea from his friend Jimmy Carter of the United States of America.

Next he seized banks and turned some of them into federal commercial banks. He seized and handed over United African Company (UAC) to Ernest Shoneka. UAC was the largest employer of direct and indirect labor in the nation

Soon, Ernest Shoneka, who managed the megacompany after the foreign owners left, ran it to the ground and retired. Millions of jobs were lost.

Contraband policy set back the hand of clock of the country's economic development for almost half a century. So sad. It affected so many businesses that so many of them went out of business. Affected also were big supermarkets, like Kingsway Stores, which the United African Company (UAC) had branches all over the country, including many other megasupermarket stores that were once the pride of the nation. Because of the contraband law, businesses could no longer import goods for their stores.

The nation's exports went into a tailspin, such as these natural products: cocoa, tin ore, palm oil, palm kernel oil, and coal. These were once the main sources of revenue for the nation before the discovery of oil. That part of the revenue sector was destroyed and uprooted because of unproductive military decrees.

Cocoa export built the western region and provided free education, water, electricity, and roads before any other region could do so. This major local export and revenue earner was abandoned due to military decrees and their fixation on the newly found oil wealth.

Businesses everywhere in the country folded. In Lagos, shops, Fortune 500 companies at Yakubu Gowon Street, Marina, King Side, Nnandi Azikewe, and Balogun Market, indeed the entire Lagos mainland markets and stores in every part of Lagos and everywhere in the nation were affected.

The nation's morning became its night, and its night became its morning. Foreign banks that were not seized pulled out of the country.

General Obasanjo perhaps didn't realize that the Nigerian-Biafra civil was over, and it was time to expand the economy, but he instead uprooted and destroyed a well-established, functioning economy that existed before he came to power. He attacked these businesses as if the Nigerian-Biafra civil war had just begun all over again. He attacked and successfully destroyed the fabric of the nation's economic market. The Nigerian masses did not buy his ideas but had no choice because he was a military head of state.

Obasanjo's Educationgate 1976

He embarked on another big surprise attack on the people of Nigeria, but this time around, it was the educational system; he hijacked private and missionary schools including higher institutions of learning. He sacked all the foreign instructors in Nigerian schools. He then invited Nigerians with PhDs from overseas and handed them over the nation's educational institutions.

These Nigerian professionals he brought home performed woefully and failed to deliver on education as anticipated. The issues of sound, quality, and quantitative education for Nigerian children were not a concern to the head of state and his administration. The nation ended up with substandard education and expired equipment. The invitees did not do the job they were invited to do which was to fix the failed educational system, rather they choose to fight each other for the rank of professorship. During this attempts some of them died mysteriously.

Obasanjo's Ban on Importation of Books

His next move was to place a ban on the importation of books. This one made me cry for the nation. I had fallen in love with a particular bookstore called CMS Bookstore, a newly completed high-rise building that harbored the biggest book collection in the country, which can be compared to Barnes & Noble of the United States of America.

Besides the bookstore, his decree hit the nation's educational system. The libraries' shelves became empty everywhere in the nation. Schools lacked textbooks and study materials.

The United African Company [UAC] and Kingsway stores once made the country proud because they offers so many things for the healthy living for Nigerians. The three most famous entities were the United African Company [UAC], Kings Ways stores and CMS bookstores but all went out of business because of indignazation, naturalization and contraband goods.

I remember vividly after he made his announcement of banning book importation, it poked the conscience of the entire nation, who rejected his idea. I remember also that some well-placed Nigerians (prominent among them was Bishop Okogi of Lagos State) pleaded to Obasanjo day in and day out not to ban books, but the adamant tyrant rejected the entreatment.

The result of his stupid follies was too hurtful to knowledge seekers in the country. The nation's educational system fell flat on its face. Bookstores folded, and the libraries and the UAC organizations folded.

His economic, political, and social decrees hit the country like the most powerful earthquake that could sweep any interfering object on its way. Meanwhile, he continued to benefit from his Otta farm while Nigerians continued to languish in poverty.

His goal was to secure his farm products and avoid competitions made him to ban all forms of imports and exports. Even something so important like food was banned

These days, whenever I visit Nigeria, I make sure I go to the sight of the CMS Bookshop. Though it is still closed for business, its memory remains. Also, this time around, I saw a little bit of life coming back to the UAC building, but on top of the building, *UAC* was written in small letters, quite unlike the old days when the same was written with the most boldest capital letters.

Obasanjo's Foreign Policy

His next move was the formation of the Nigerian National Institute of International Affairs. He appointed Boliji Akinyemi as its director general. It soon became a hub for African tyrant leaders who gathered to rant against the West; they apparently appeared to be confused. The Cold War was raging, the apartheid in South Africa was on, and the unlawful, unjust, and immoral military overthrow of lawful governments in almost every African country was a big problem and was growing.

Hints of wars in some of the African nations were heard. Normal daily lives were disrupted in almost everywhere in Africa.

Western nations' investments were uprooted and destroyed without any means of replacing them. Unemployment, hunger, and disease multiplied in all of these nations. The introduction of green revolution, austerity and belt tightening measures were counterproductive because them did not make a dent in the economy or neither creates jobs, it was obnoxious fraud.

But his real agenda was to own Nigeria and make sure that nobody challenges his ruthless and useless social and economic decrees against the country. He succeeded beyond all reasonable doubt in his bid to squander his nation's potential.

Contributing to this madness were the 1 percent narcissist elite, who thought that they could control the masses, and also the power-drunk self-appointed so-called African heads of state who ruined Africa by socially and economically enslaving African citizens in the name of African unity.

It was mayhem in Africa in those days. It was like to live or not live, to be or not to be. Indeed African people were truly stressed out because of the tyrant manner of these leaders. Everything fell apart, jobs, businesses, education, health care, name them.

Why Africa Failed

Soon the African heads of state gathered for a meeting under the Organization of African Unity (OAU). At the end of the meeting, a statement was issued to inform Africans citizens and the world that they had adopted African foreign policy known as the African Nonally Movement (ANAM). The reason according to them was the Cold War because the African nations did not want to specifically tie themselves to either the West's or the East's warring factions. The African leaders' proposals backfired and hurt African nations' economic development for years.

The idea that an entire continent will put their foreign policy in one basket was deadly wrong. It was a costly mistake, a very expensive malady. Only the citizens of these nations paid the highest price for such shortsightedness on foreign relationship.

Each and every member of the Organization of African Unity is said to be Republic and Democratic, so why would any of these nations allow their nation to be controlled with a remote control and be told not to interact personally with other nations of their choice?

Tell African citizens the names of those who coined the phrase *nonally movement*. The African non-ally movement, I believed achieved its objective of been neutral during the cold war but at what cost to their economy?

There was no specific role the African nations could have played if a third world war was started but any of the waring super powers, West or East, would have seized any of these African nations and forced them to fight on their side. The First and Second World War were classic examples of what could have happened to African nations if there was a world war because no amount of nonally movement could have saved them from joining the war at one side of the war theater just like previous World Wars.

The African general's and head of states squandered their potentials when they uprooted foreign investments.

No one can tell the reasons behind the seizing and uprooting of foreign businesses by African leaders in their countries. Its economic impact is too much to mention. This economic policy devastated their economic progress for years. This action resulted was been classified as "failed states."

Instead of educating armies of professionals, inventors, creators, scientists, and producers to help the economic decrees enacted in the 70s and 80s downgraded nation's economically.

The military intrudetion into politics created the biggest economic crisis that is still affects the nation social, economic and political growth.

Everyone knew that during the apartheid era, the continent joined forces to speak with one voice against its evil, but that does not translate into one foreign policy to fit the entire continent and wouldn't be an excuse for uprooting and destroying existing infrastructure left behind by the colonial masters, which would have served as a stepping stone for more economic developments for these nations.

Instead of these nations thinking and mapping out longtime future economic goals with the help of the existing infrastructures, they chose to uproot and destroy them without other means to replace them for the sake of their people. That economic foundation laid down by the colonial masters was destroyed.

The Head of Nigerian Institute of International Affairs

During Bolaji Akinyemi's time as the head of the Nigerian Institute of International Affairs, Nigerians could still remember that any time he appeared on the national TV, he was always a bad-news bearer. In those days, he was denouncing one foreign nation or another. He would step up to inform the nation about another nationalization of foreign investments, which was always at the detriment of that nation's economic future, and the masses were usually the ones who paid the price.

One thing the economic decree makers didn't realize was that these businesses that were nationalized were not owned by foreign governments but rather were owned by individual foreign investors who invested their money in these nations and helped to create jobs and better lives for Nigerians until the government took it away from the rightful owners.

Perhaps, the decree makers' aim was to deal with their perceived enemies, but instead, they penalized their nations by attacking foreign businesses as their weapons of mass destruction to get even with the West. This was their brand of cold war, to uproot international investments in their respective countries, and so they subjected their people to years of untold economic hardships that haven't ended yet.

No one is against African unity, but it shouldn't be purely on politics or wars against its own people. What African nations need today are social and economic development jobs, opportunities, education, health care, roads, water, and electricity, not disease and hunger.

The foreign policies enacted by African heads of state in the late seventies and eighties no doubt downgraded their ability to develop free market enterprises.

The African leaders who uprooted their nation's economy cannot compare that they did to Nelson Mandela's dreams of a rainbow nation. He spent twenty-seven years of his life in jail. When he came out, he was not only smarter but also was far more sophisticated politically, socially, and economically than those African leaders who led African nations to economic and social ruins.

Nelson Mandela, the World Statesman

For the love of his nation and people, he endured twenty-seven years of punishing jail time. He came out of prison without showing any bitterness and buried the hatchet. He was stronger and wiser.

Paramount in his heart was the future of his nation; he dreamed of a better South Africa in particular and Africa in general as well as the world. He thanked those nations and individuals and South African citizens who sacrificed to secure his freedom from prison and the granting of freedom to every South African citizen.

He forgave his tormentors and initiated the Truth and Reconciliation Commission and appointed no other person than the indomitable Archbishop Desmond Tutu as the chairman of the board.

Its purpose was to bring peace, harmony, and togetherness for all South Africans, both black and white. He was easily elected the first black president of South Africa. He ran the country with the best of his ability, knowledge, skills, and passion.

Bishop Desmond Tutu was the first to use the term *rainbow nation*, which is described as a dream for the unity of all South Africans no matter what the color. Based on this knowledge, he understood the task before him and never disappointed the people of South Africa as the chairman of the board. A good job was done. Deeds and their inspiration that made Nelson Mandela and Desmond Tutu statesmen and industrious sons of Africa. They are huge inspirations to what leaders in African should aspire to follow the leadership examples of Nelson Mandala. After the death of our leader Nelson Mandela, we must never forget him.

Mandela and Tutu refused to succumb to the mean-spirited act of indigenization, nationalization, and privatization of international businesses. Instead, they preserved the country together for a greater South Africa that will be there for all South Africans.

Mandela could have chosen to remain in power until his death, just like many African leaders did. Instead, after four years of laying a very strong foundation for a better South Africa, he called it quits and yielded power to the next generation of South Africans of all credo.

He became a statesman not by choice but by his deeds. He is beloved by everyone.

The African nations must continue to honor this great African statesman and of the world by establishing a departmental chair of Nelson Mandela leadership and government in universities all over Africa.

Every day I pray for South Africa because my fear is whether they will keep the spirit and the work of Nelson Mandela intact or if they will take the same highway like the less of the African nations took after attaining independence. I sincerely hope that it will never happen.

My fears have been arrayed, knowing that Archbishop Tutu has not given up preaching his ideal of a rainbow nation for all South

Africans in particular and Africa in general. Though much work is still needed to be done, with diligence, love, trust, peace, and harmony, it could be done. Tutu, who is a prolific writer, has written so many books on the future of South Africans and Africans, which are must read. Some of his books are *The Book of Forgiveness* and *An African Prayer*, which are quite inspiring. There are other books.

The African Union Formation

Has anyone ever asked whether the African Union Organization is the most pressing need for African nations today? This organization was primarily responsible for the downfall of African economies. Majority of African nations are barely under sixty years of existence but seems in a hurry to reach the goals that took the Europeans hundreds of years to accomplish.

The African leaders deliberately uprooted and destroyed the critical infrastructures left behind by their colonial masters, undermining economy growth in these nations. It was the biggest mistake made that none of these nations has been able to fix, which has left them underdeveloped.

The European Union

For example, each member nation of the European Union have existed for at least a minimum of one hundred years and has achieved advanced economies. Also, no self-proclaimed leader in Europe single-handedly formed the European Union undemocratically, as it was the case when the African Union was formed by a few drunk leaders. Rather, Europe used referendum to achieve its objective of creating the European Union.

At the beginning, to achieve their objectives. The first balloting failed, and the second balloting took place, which finally sailed through, hence the birth of the European Union. The union members have a strong economy with advanced development, and they are also wealthy nations, unlike the African Union, who forgot the basics.

The union was formed by and then imposed it on African citizens.

The union is often kept under the foot mat of the most brutal African dictatorial leaders who finance it. An example was Libyan dictator Muammar Gaddafi, who without doubt was its chief financier.

The urgent needs of African nations today are nothing but economic, social, and political reforms! Reforms that will serve as means to rebuild their critical infrastructures shattered and destroyed by their despotic leaders. A union that seems to have nothing to offer in terms of economic development should wait. Africans are tired of playing dirty politics that does no one good. They want to see jobs and better lives in their various nations, not more politics.

Each and every African nation should start reforms that should begin from the top down, and everything must be on the table, and nothing will be spared. It should be a quest to begin to build better African nations that will be accessible to their people with respect to the rules of law to protect everyone's rights.

The time has come when the old political order must be let go in every African nation. African leaders must stop squandering their potentials through mismanaging of their resources, which led to their inability to create jobs and opportunities for their people. These economic situations are the causes why many young men and women in these nations are fleeing their countries in search of greener pastures abroad.

African nations can boast a trunkful of talented, skilled, and creative people, but because of ignorance in politics, which lead to bribery and corruptions, they are ignored and wasted, and they go unrecognized and unused, making these nations to remain undeveloped. Actions are required now and not later to save these nations from further disintegration.

The African Union can be disbanded for now and could wait until maybe the next fifty years, when most African nations would have attained economic growth and progress and become well-developed economies. They should pursue technology. At least for now these nations can go their separate ways to enable each and every one of them to reform their various nations first and foremost. They should strive to make use of their potentials to rebuild their shattered economies for this to establish a new era. The old established political orders should be dismantled bit by bit until they no longer exist.

The African Union will be advised to initiate a balloting referendum for African people to vote yes or no if the African Union will continue or not. This union should take a cue from the Europeans that in the name of democracy, they require an approval from African member nations through balloting if they want to remain as a continental union.

When Mikhail Gorbachev, the last czar of the Soviet Union, came to power, he wasn't pleased with what he saw about the union's economy, which led to changes and finally to the dissolution of the Warsaw Pact. Today, it has served former member states who were chained together to one of the most unprogressive state economies in the world at that period.

Africa/China

There couldn't have been no doubt whether Nigeria or any other African nation could have been like the China of today because they both have the same cheap labor market. At the time the West was looking for places to manufacture their products cheaply, the African nations had closed its doors against themselves by their use of nonally movement doctrine and purposefully uprooting and destroying some well-established critical infrastructures in their nations. The true story was that the African Union nonally movement wasn't structured to enhance the economic, social, and security needs of the union members, hence they supported the uprooting and destroying of international businesses as well as expelling business owners and their foreign workers from Africa. Their actions were purely apolitical. The most affected were the African masses, who had no voice to oppose their leaders but ended paying the biggest price for this type of African foreign policy that left their economy shattered, creating massive unemployment. Now the same African despotic leaders are begging China to invest in their countries.

Where were the African Union and African leaders in the 1999 World Global Economic Forum? Towards the end of the forum, the prime minister of Singapore was asked to propose the fate of Africa in the twenty-first century world global economy. Here is what he said, "Africa should not be included in the world global economy because they will be a drag." I waited for a response from the African Union, African leaders, and African elites, but none of them ever responded to this accusation made against their nations. Sadly enough, none of them responded. Their pastime these days is to go around the world making noise and refusing to tell themselves the truth about what is going on in their nations, their misrules.

The same reasons the African Union and African leaders had in the seventies to eighties are the same reasons they have today for not joining the world global economy: because of their confused idea of nonallied movement. They choose to move backward instead of forward so as to continue to enslave their own people socially and economically by ripping them off of their collective wealth.

Promoting bribery and corruption and downgrading their nations' economies and creating massive economic disadvantages, lower-class and underclass citizens while only 1 percent of the citizens control the people's wealth. The only solution to the continental problems is nothing but *political socializations* to sack all established old politicians who have ruined the continent with their misrule and misdeed and corruption. At the turn of the century, it is the hour that the masses of Africa will use a Martin Luther King Jr. type of nonviolent revolution to reclaim their nations to end the political, economic, and social injustice, corruptions, and immoral leaderships.

Obasanjo, Military Head of State, Ended 1979

At the end of his four-year term, General Obasanjo conducted a democratic election both for the presidency and governorship, the national assembly and state assemblies. Once again, it was more of a tribal divide than a national characteristic election. Notable among prominent Nigerian politicians who contested the election were Nnamdi Azikiwe, Awolowo, Aminu Kano, A. Ogunsanja, and others. These men are the architects of Nigerian independence. Included was Shehu Shagari, a newcomer to the political arena. At the end of the election, Shehu Shagari was declared the winner. The outgoing head of state, General Obasanjo, successfully transferred power to the new head of state. After which, he moved to his new home, the Otta farm, while leaving behind for the new president truckloads of social, political, and economic problems. He created and abandoned these problems for the new president.

President Shagari Regime, 1979–1983

Shagari was a good man, a very nice guy, a God-fearing man, probably beyond corruption. Along with the national assembly members, they couldn't identify the enormous economic, political, and social problems facing the nation, talk less of finding solutions—a carry-over from Obasanjo's regime. If he had undone the unproductive indigenization and nationalization of international businesses by his predecessors, the nation's economy would have once again come to life. Nigerians were mad because they were losing their jobs and businesses, and he did nothing about it.

Though he was a good man, he presided over one of the most corrupted administrations in the nation's history. Government buildings were touched after embezzlements, frauds, and stealing multiplied and became a habit and was no longer a secret, and the penetrators openly lived lavishly. Notable among the buildings touched were the Independent Building and the Nigerian National Telecommunication Building, which are counted among some of Nigeria's tallest buildings. In the heat of all these, he became a candidate for removal, and it wasn't difficult for General Buhari to shove him aside because the nation was already tired of his administration.

General Buhari Regime, Head of State, 1983–1985

Soon General Buhari staged his coup and shoved President Shagari out of power with the greatest relief for Nigerians. Nigerians were really happy to see the Shagari government go. Buhari was welcomed with open minds by Nigerians. At first it seemed to look like he was the messiah Nigerians had been waiting for had finally arrived. He came with such a big bang that he elicited such hope that Nigerians were looking forward to a better future after the Obasanjo and Shagari failures. He lay emphasis on public order and discipline, leading to the birth of Sanitation Day. But instead of creating jobs, he jumped into another nationalization of international investment by seizing and changing the name of British Petroleum to African Petroleum, which did not go down well with Nigerians. Soon Nigerians got fed up with him because they didn't appreciate his leadership style. Besides that, Buhari is good and a nice man who loves his country. He was not corrupt, and he wanted to tackle the issue of bribery and corruption, but he failed due to his method of approach in tackling the problems. He misjudged Nigerians, especially those he employed as aides, who undermine all his efforts by giving him bad advices on the state of things in the nation. He appears to grasp what the nation's trolley problems were, but he was short on fixing it because little effort was made on creating jobs and opportunities. He hired bad advisers, those who told him what he wanted to hear and not what he wanted know to take the nation to the right direction. As a result, his government failed.

General Babangida, 1985–1993

Nigerians nicknamed him the Diego Maradona, the Evil Genius, and the Gambler.

Nigerians witnessed yet another government overthrow. This time it was Babangida overthrowing General Buhari. The time he was removed from office was ripe because Nigerians had lost confidence in the ability of Buhari to lead the country. He was no longer the perceived reformer or the anticipated messiah that Nigerians expected. So it was easy for Babangida to remove him. Clearly, Nigerians had no choice and no say over the issue of military coup after military coup in the country. It has become a national disgrace and shame. As usual, when Babangida took power, Nigerians once again applauded him for getting off their neck another military leader and government. Nigerians were relieved and felt some air of freedom for those few months or years of Buhari's regime

General Babangida's Introduction of Second-Tier Market

By the time the nation's new chief executive completed his power takeover, the nation's social and economic situation was already on life support and at a point of putting the final nail on the nation's economic coffin.

But the only solution the chief executive and his finance minister came up with was the second-tier initiative. From day one, I was opposed to it because I knew that it was not the right prescription for the nation's economic woes caused by Nigerian leaders. The Nigerian naira was stronger than the US dollar; it was fifty kobo to one dollar before the second-tier initiative. Indeed, Nigerian currency, I fear, will never be the same again and that it will hit the point of no return. It was a systematic devaluation of the naira. The result was further damage to an already very sick and weak economy; it was an imposed murder on Nigerian currency, no doubt about it.

The good days are gone. This is an oil-rich nation. The problem was lack of management skills, bad economic decrees after bad economic decrees enacted by the nation's self-appointed leaders and aided by their chosen fly-by-night economists who were appointed finance ministers. Most of them studied abroad and had PhDs. The most simple, basic thing these presidents should have done was to revoke and undo the indigenization and nationalization of foreign businesses and lift the trade embargoes decreed by the previous administrations; if this was done, it would have brought the economy back to normal.

But instead they decreed more stupid and meaningless economic disasters that crashed the economy and robbed Nigerians of their way of life and means of living.

The government refuses to reform the economy. The military decrees were set to destroy the country economically and socially, which was exactly the result today. They preferred to unleash the greatest economic and social hardship on Nigerians. The question should be whether the decrees' purposes were solely meant to hurt the foreign businesses or to hurt Nigerians.

ACB Bank Manager, Second-Tier Market

I remember my heated argument with a friend of mine who was an ACB bank manager then. When I gave him a candid advice to pay his child's school fees overseas, he refused, telling me that he had many years of experience as a bank manager and that the naira will beat the dollar thirty kobo to one dollar at the start of the second-tier market. I told him that he was daydreaming, that it wasn't going to happen, and that the naira is finished and will never be the same again.

On the first day of the second-tier market bidding, the dollar equalized naira one to one. I went back to him to again tell him to pay the school fees now. He told me to get lost, that he has been a bank manager for twenty years, that he was very confident that the naira will rise to thirty kobo against the dollar at next week's bidding. I told him he was kidding me because it will never happen.

He disbelieved me but continued to hope that somehow the naira will beat the dollar by thirty kobo to one dollar; at which time he will pay the school fees for his child studying in America, but that never happened The second week of the second-tier market, the naira jumped to four naira to one US dollar.

Today in Nigeria, the naira is hovering against the US dollar at almost 190 naira to 1 dollar, more than a 200 percent increase. Those school fees were never paid. My prediction that this economic measure will go down in the history book of Nigeria as one of the worst economic policies ever decreed in this country and that it will ruin this nation's economy for years to come has come true. Finally, my friend was never able to pay his child's school fees because the exchange rate had shot up beyond his reach, and he was no longer able to afford the payment. Finally, second-tier did my friend in. His bank, ACB Bank, went under, and he lost his job. So sad it happened.

General Babangida possesses such a powerful personality with his full-toothed smiles that many Nigerians just love him regardless of whatever he does. His leadership was like see no evil, hear no evil, and speak no evil. You can break the law if you can, except do not overthrow him. Today, the naira still remains in a dump. Almost twenty-seven years after, the currency continues to fluctuate badly and makes life very difficult for many Nigerians. Day-by-day existence is a big struggle for many in the country.

The Four Economic Decrees That Finished the Nation

They are the second-tier, the indigenization, the nationalization, and the trade restrictions economic decrees and its consequences on the nation. It created great deals of economic and social havoc on Nigerian people's well-beings. As a matter of fact, everything came to a standstill for years in the country.

Consequences

1. Parents and guardians were no longer able to pay their children's school fees abroad; the transitions for these students were painful.
2. So many banks went under, including my friend's bank, African Continental Bank [ACB].
3. There was a third round of job losses; the Nigerian middle class became the last class.
4. Businesses suffered and many closed down all over the federation, especially Lagos, the Nigerian center of commerce. Broad Street, Balogun Market were almost emptied.
5. Many more Nigerians could not even afford a meal a day.
6. Inflation went sky high.
7. Movie theaters shut down all over the country. Nigerians still remember God-dey Cinema at Olodi Apapa in Lagos; the most modern theater house in the country shunted its doors for good due to a ban on importation. This past January 2014 that I visited Nigeria, I passed through the former theater house, and it has been turned into a junkyard.
8. Nigerian days became their nights and days became their nights. A society that once operated twenty-four hours every day now closes its doors at 6:00 p.m.
9. The mass exodus of Nigerian men and women fleeing the country to escape poverty and hardship escalated, and it was like to flee to any another country but not Nigeria. Many lost their lives in the process to escape poverty and hardship in their country. It was a dog-eat-dog kind of life in the country.
10. Once one of the most respected countries in the world became known as a criminal nation. The economic decrees

had completely revised the utilitarian theory of creating the greatest happiness for the greatest number of people to creating the greatest happiness for the shortest number of people. All these led to escalation of crime in the nation.

11. By the 1990s, the living condition had reached the lowest. Food were scarce, and essential commodities were difficult to come by, except if you were a very, very rich person.

Added to these problems was the daily commute. It was difficult because vehicles left in the country were old and rickety buses and cars that were beyond repair due to lack of motor parts. The theme those days was "My foot run" because everyone walked. In the seventies, this was a nation where if you had four or five thousand naira, you could walk into any car dealer shop, pay, and drive out with a brand-new car. The value of the same amount today in US dollars is about seven to eight thousand, but it cannot buy you a decent used car.

The contraband policy devastated the economy. Nigerians became smugglers to help prevent the country from a sudden economic collapse because the country did not produce anything. The Nigerian leaders did not have any clue about the havoc their economic decrees were causing the nation. And they were creating massive poverty and unemployment among the people. Despite all these failures, they continued doing the same mistake over and over.

The men and women who took to smuggling to bring in needed products to save the country from economic collapse were very courageous people because they often lost their money and goods if caught by customs, who will in thus convert the seized property to themselves. Though smuggling is a criminal act, there was no way out for Nigerians. They must do whatever they can to survive because there was no other choice.

For the past forty years that ban on import decrees has been in force, the economic cost to Nigerians and the government may have come close to more than five hundred billion US Dollars in custom's revenue to smugglers and to the custom officers themselves, the immigration officers, the police officers.

My Encounter with the Nigerian Police Force

In 1994, I visited Nigeria. I boarded one of the available rickety cars traveling from Lagos to the east of the nation to visit my family. At Benin, halfway to my destination, we ran into a police roadblock right in the center of the highway and were pulled over and ordered to disembark. We obeyed. They began the frisking of passengers first and then moved to search passengers' personal belongings; at which point they found four pairs of shoes in my bag and demanded I explain how I got four pairs of shoes and what my job was.

The police officers became jealous of my shoes and ordered the driver and my copassengers to continue the trip without me, but both the driver and the passengers refused to leave without me. To my greatest surprise, every one of the passengers and the driver sat down on the ground, vowing not to leave without me. I had never met Nigerians that were so nice and good in my life; these passengers were more than courageous, great Nigerians, my heroes.

Inside the bag they found the shoes, I had a large sum of money well hidden in such a way that it cannot be easily be detected by anyone else except me because I was warned about police tactics of robbing and killing innocent passengers, especially Nigerians returning from abroad with money. I was told that police officers have formed the habit of robbing returning Nigerians of their money and possessions and then turned around and killed them.

I soon understood the reason behind my copassengers' and the driver's refusal not to leave without me was because they knew what the consequences would have been if they had left without me. They knew that I will never come out alive in the hands of these police officers because they will kill me just because of four pairs of shoes and perhaps locate the money in the bag. The economic situation in the nation was in such a bad state and shape that some Nigerian police officers became armed bandits in official government uniforms to survive the harsh economic climate in the country then. After detaining us for more than thirty minutes and realizing that no passenger would budge to leave me behind, they had no choice but to release us, and we drove away. I will always be grateful to those courageous Nigerians who saved my life in the hands of Nigerian police officers.

It is a well-documented fact that the police officers have killed so many Nigerians returning from America and Europe who had money and goods on them at the police roadblocks found all over the country. They were mounted to menace their fellow citizens and hid under government official uniforms.

Guess what, do you know of a reasonable government anywhere in the world that will clog their express roads, highways, and streets with police checkpoints, customs checkpoints, immigration checkpoints, traffic wardens checkpoints, mobile police checkpoints, military checkpoints, and road safety checkpoints? And every day in the nation, new ones are formed to harass and rob their fellow citizens. The Nigerian authorities who created these agencies turned the nation into a police state that made life hell for the citizens.

Did the Nigerian government create these numerous checkpoints for law enforcement agencies to harass and collect bribes and deprive the masses their possessions on a daily basis? The situation in Nigeria was similar to that of gangs of New York in the 1800s, but Nigerian faction is the worst. However, while the masses sweat it out, the other 1 percent rich Nigerians continue to enjoy life and get richer and richer by stealing and pocketing the people's collective wealth. All these was possible because of the unproductive economic decrees that was put in place to favor the rich.

New Capital Abuja

As naive as the government leaders may be, even though they cannot give account of the whereabouts of the nation's oil wealth, they went ahead to squander much of the remaining money in the name of building a new capital called Abuja, a no-man's-land at the time.

The Nigerian government is always interested in initiating elephant projects in order to waste and steal the people's wealth. Over 70 percent of the Abuja capital budget expenditure was stolen by individuals. The prime real estates part of the town was hijacked by well-heeled Nigerians and top government officials, who built luxurious houses and shopping plazas. They boldly hijacked the people's wealth and prime real estates and built a city where even the nation's professionals can't afford to live because they can't afford the high rent and landlords' demand of two to three years' rent advanced payment. The city was built and reserved for Nigerian rouge leaders. Indeed, Nigerians were robbed in broad day light by their leaders and their cronies, whom they entrusted with their destinies.

The Conversion of Prime Real Estates by the Few Rich in Abuja

In the end, Nigerians did not get a modern capital. There is no running clean water, no electricity, no modern sinkholes, no housing for the masses. Instead, they were sent to the undeveloped portion of the capital to live. Most parts of the capital still use old toilet pits for their hygiene. Definitely, these struggling Nigerians were priced out of the opportunity to live and share the main town of Abuja with the rich.

"The time has arrived when patience becomes a crime and mayhem appears garbed in the mantle of virtue" (Philander in icy tones). It is time to peacefully uproot, destroy, and rebuild, rebuild, bigger, better, and stronger. It is time for change. It is time for them to go and leave Nigeria for Nigerians. The Nigerians' patience has run out, and it is time for action. Absolutely, Abuja will be reassessed and rebuilt should Nigerians elect a visionary new government to power in 2015, which I urge Nigerians to consider if they want a better life for themselves and their families. Abuja right now is built only for the rich Nigerians. And it is wrong to send the masses to live in the "Siberian" part of the city, and it is not acceptable.

The government must set up a board of inquiries to investigate the Abuja "Shoppingplazagates" and the "Luxuryhousesgates" that dominate the entire city. About 80 percent of them should be replaced in order to make way to develop critical infrastructures to jump-start the economy. Schools, hospitals, public housing, local offices, and many others should replace these non-revenue-earning and non-job-creating ventures owned by the rich.

The government can evoke its reserved eminent demean power to reclaim these lands because they are needed for building critical infrastructures to create jobs and opportunities for Nigerians.

Abiola Elected President: Never to Be?

After he ripped off Nigerians left and right, he even had the nerve to want to be their president. He was a senior accountant with International Telephone Telegraph (ITT) when during the indigenization period, he was handed over the keys to the company after the owners were forced to leave. He milked the company dry and abandoned it, and that was the end of ITT as Nigerians know it. His influence and popularity began the day the keys to the company were given to him. A popular and well-known musician, Fela, wrote a song to portray his failure to manage and keep the company functioning. He instead stole the money left behind by the former foreign owners. The song goes like this: "Abiola, ITT thief, ITT thief, and thief, thief, thief." How can he run a business if he did not have access to its intellectual property, technical knowledge? He had no finances and lacked the management skill to run a Fortune 500 company. His next target was the military. Somehow he warmed his heart to the military officers and began to win uncontested contracts from the military boys, which made him millions of naira and made him to become one of the richest men in Nigeria. He should have remained a businessman instead of running for president; that caused him his life. I am sorry that he ended his life in his attempt to be a president. No one deserved to die in the name of politics.

Ernest Shonekan's Presidency, 1993

There was no doubt about it: his service with the United African Company (UAC), which I greatly admired, merits praise. He rose to the top echelons of his career due to hard work. I would like to know what his thoughts are about the indigenization and nationalization in Nigeria as a captain of a giant industry and how he felt about the trade embargoes decrees that ended his company. I wonder if he has written any book on these issues. However, due to the indigenization decree, he was handed over the keys to UAC because its British owners were forced to leave. But by the time he retired, a once-giant company was already on life support. At least one of the signature branches of the company, the Kingsway Stores, had folded, and numerous other UAC branches followed suit, and soon the main head office joined in closing. That was the end of UAC as Nigerians knew it. A giant company that created millions of direct and indirect jobs for Nigerians was used as toilet roll because of a reckless military decree.

After an inconclusive election that would have made Abiola the next president of Nigeria failed, he was invited to serve as an interim president pending resolution of the matter. His acceptance of this mandate to serve as a temporary president and the actions he took after that looked something like an act of cowardice, and it baffled Nigerians. The nation was set on fire due to the inconclusive election, and he was called to take over the government, and after completing the takeover of power, he told Nigerians that he was going to London in search of a solution. You may ask, "What solution? You are the solution now!" Many Nigerians thought that it was an act of cowardice because cowards die many times before their death, or he didn't want to hurt his kin, Abiola. While he was still in the air en route to London in search of a solution, General Abacha sent a message to him that he needed not come back because the office of the president was no longer available. General Abacha had taken over the office of the president. Based on this, Shonekan's presidential euphoria ended abruptly. Bearing this in mind, Nigerians do not know if he is qualified to be called a former Nigerian president. He never performed any known official duty or formulated any known governmental policy during his short time in office.

General Abacha, Head of State, 1993–1998

All he wanted was to be a Nigerian president at all costs. He was supposed to have retired along with his boss, but he ducked behind because of his evil desire to be president. He was a lame duck president and no-nonsense human being. Nigerians were informed that he enriched himself, his family, and some close family friends fabulously with billions of US dollars stolen from Nigerians

He was a tough person and not a tough sensible leader because there was no tangible achievement to show during his time in office as a president. His mood means, "Do not cross me." His government was for Abacha and Abacha and all for Abacha. But he succeeded where others failed by getting tough with Obasanjo and sending him to the cooler. Abacha knows too well about the touching of the Independent Building during his time there, when a massive looting occurred in the building that led to it being touched.

How to Fix Nigeria?

I have made an attempt to point out the genesis of Nigerian problems and those Nigerian leaders that caused the problems. The next discourse will be on how Nigerian future leaders can return the country back to its political, social, and economic stability once again and put Nigerians back to work. Recently I visited Nigeria. What I saw was quite disgraceful, something not befitting of an oil-rich country that swims in oil dough. I cannot believe that Nigerian masses would be benefiting from all kinds of junk goods lifted from Dumpsters from cities of European countries. It is beyond the expired technology they usually benefited from. Junks brought home from Europe are a big market because the people have no choice. Nigeria has become the dumping ground for Europe's discarded household items including junk vehicles of all types and makes with serious emission problems.

Why is this happening? It is because of a stupid economic policy banning the importation of goods that the nation cannot produce, making the masses not have a choice but to patronize these junks brought into the country illegally. Why are the nation's leaders choosing to be penny-wise and pound-foolish? While the lame duck executive branch, the president, the lame duck rubber stamp national assembly members, the lame duck state governors, and the lame duck rubber stamp state assembly members are given brand-new cars, brand-new mansions, free medical care for themselves and families abroad, free education for their children abroad, and the benefit of brand-new items from abroad for their personal use, buying mansions and investing in overseas stock markets with stolen Nigerian money while the masses bite the dust in order to exist and fetch for their families.

The homes of Nigerian leaders, families, and friends are equipped with the most expensive generators for light while the masses live in darkness on a daily basis.

Junk Goods

It still remains as a big shame that an oil-rich nation is only benefitting from junks lifted from the streets of European Dumpsters and exported to Nigeria as used goods These junks goods are then sold in every nook and corner of the country as imported goods. It is basically what the masses can afford in this present time of economic hardship in the nation. Would anyone blame Nigerians who patronize these junks or neither blame those who brought them home? These junks are what the masses can find and can afford. For more than thirty-seven years, the federal government has placed a ban on the importation of foreign goods, so these junks get smuggled into the country and it helps to sustain the nation's economy. Added to hyperinflations and higher naira exchange rates, it is difficult to make ends meet.

Public Conveniences

Fifty-four years after independence, the nation still suffers from endemic power failures, lack of jobs, lack of clean water, lack of roads, lack of health care, lack of security, lack of quality education, and so on and so forth. The biggest question to ask is, where is the oil money? Why did the rich 1 percent of Nigerians and foreigners hijack the oil money to themselves? Government officials of all classes choose embezzlement of the people's wealth instead of investing it to benefit everyone.

Obasanjo's Elected President, 1999–2007

General Abacha had jailed Obasanjo during his regime. He was still in lockup at the time of Abacha's death. Somehow after Abacha died, he was sprung out from jail by his cronies and set free, but that is the way the Nigerian criminal justice system works. The law is broken with careless abandon. Nigerians have always believed that Obasanjo's leadership was a curse on Nigeria as a punishment for overthrowing General Gowon.

In the midst of confusion arising from the election of Abiola and its rejection by the military leaders, a new election was called for. Obasanjo soon will join the pack of presidential contenders. How he got the money to finance his presidential campaign after less than a month after coming out of jail is still on known. Of course, there is no record to show how Nigerian politicians pay for their campaign funding, though billions of naira exchanges hand in the name of bribery and corruptions. One day, as Nigerians progressively mature and become more sophisticated politically, the same questions will be asked again, and perhaps the answers on how Nigerian politicians finance their campaigns and their sources will be known. For now it still remains a secret to Nigerian watchers. No elected politician in the country will have the nerve to claim that Nigerians elected him officially to the office he or she is holding or has held in the past.

The international election monitors may tell you that the election was free and fair. That is what they thought. How will they account for missing ballot boxes after the election and stuffed ballot boxes that favor those that the powerful want to be elected?

After the 1999 general elections, news reached me that Obasanjo had been named the winner of the presidential election. My first reaction was to ask why. And I cried for Nigerians. It was another sad day of yet another political darkness to engulf the nation once again. Did Nigerians forget how Obasanjo brought down the nation's economy and left it in tatters before retiring? On further inquiries as to the reasons leading to the election of Obasanjo, I was told that Nigerians never, never elected Obasanjo, that he was rigged into power that they had no power to stop. Those powerful men and women who rigged Obasanjo into power know themselves, and Nigerians know them. They are still alive today.

Having settled down to accept Obasanjo as the president of Nigeria, my immediate thought was about some urgent issues that he needed to address if he wanted to be a successful president this time around:

a. Can he reverse himself?
b. Can he recognize his previous backwards decrees?
c. Can he hire those who will look him directly in his face and tell him the bitter truth? (Sir, you must reverse yourself for the good of the country. Sir, this nation cannot achieve any meaningful growth without reforms, reforms, and reforms.)

As I continued to monitor the situation, the news came that he has hired Ngozi Okonjo-Iweala from the World Bank to be his finance minister. I said, "Good omen. God bless him." I thought it was a perfect catch and good thing for the nation and a good way to start fixing the nation's economy and creating jobs.

As the newly minted finance minister took her chair at the finance ministry, I was full of hope that the country will see some noticeable economic changes that will bring jobs back. One thing I had hoped to hear from the economic minister was about her strategic plans to restore economic stability in the nation. I have expected her to read the economic riot act to her boss by addressing him boldly and directly, "Sir, the only answer to the country's current economic problems is to undergo top to bottom reforms and nothing but reforms and reforms. I thought that coming from the world and as a World Bank insider, she could employ the help of the bank to help the nation effect economic reforms since she will be less suspicious than someone else doing it. I waited for the first year—nothing. On the second year nothing happened. On the third year nothing happened. We got lost in a limbo waiting for her to pronounce that magic word of *reforms* and *downsize*, but it never came.

I expected her to tell her boss to reverse his previous economic military style decrees that left the nation's economy in tatters or at least help to end the contraband decrees that is hurting Nigerians. But the bad news to Nigerians was that she is a fan of trade protectionism, meaning that the doors for foreign partnership will close and will not allow the lifting of trade barriers. While the country continues to lose billions and billions of dollars of custom duties and levies to private individual pockets and neighboring countries, the nation's treasurer is left holding the empty bag. The fact and the truth is that she and the president including everybody else in the nation depend on the contraband goods for their daily needs, therefore making everybody, including her and the president, to be lawbreakers, criminals, and smugglers. People may wonder, Why should a nation that does not produce a pin place an economic sanction on itself? How does the government expect to stabilize the economy if everybody in the nation is made a smuggler? If you are not a smuggler, you will buy smuggled goods. For the masses to benefit from these smuggled goods, the nation has become a dumping ground for inexpensive junk goods lifted from Dumpsters in Europe in the name of goods and smuggled into the country. Is this the way visionary leaders operate? I doubt.

Obasanjo Went Back to His Old Tricks, Privatizations

Not done with causing injuries and massive economic failures in the nation, he and his finance minister introduced another dubious, evil design public policy but this time rechristened it privatizations. This was another tactic to deprive Nigerians of their legally owned prime real estates, corporations, and oil wells that will once again be passed over to the haves and well connected in the nation!

It could have been a shock to Nigerians when they heard that the president and his finance minister are selling off the nation's high-price real estates and corporations to the highest bidder and mostly the rich while the masses languished in poverty and hunger. Nobody knew the roles the members of the Nigerian national congress played in all these or whether they authorized the president and his finance minister to embark on this unlawful and unjust sale of the best, most luxurious, expensive real estates and corporations and oil wells owned by the Nigerians.

The president and his finance minister would have known that it was wrong to sell these properties without reforms first. Those reforms should have been considered first and been given center stage and should have allowed Nigerians to have a say and ask for their input in the matter at the national level, where they will join to decide whether to sell or not to sell. Their actions should be considered as a broad-day robbery of the people's assets because of their failure to reform the nation's economy before embarking on yet another destructive economic policy. They continued with their choice of wrong and dubious economic misdirections that hurt the people's way of life.

In Nigeria the law is made by the superior for the inferior to obey. Who cares about laws? The most troubling fact about all these is that Nigerians have pinned their hope on the lady from the World Bank to help the country reach economic stability and return them back to workforce, but she failed the people. First, she supported the trade embargo that was introduced by her boss, Obasanjo, and has been in place for thirty-eight years. Ever since then, it has been hurting the economy, hurting Nigerians, and putting millions of Nigerians out of work. The government loses billions of dollars in revenue to the so-called smugglers and the neighboring countries who do not have trade embargo in their nations. The Nigerian government also loses billions of dollars in custom duties to the neighboring countries where Nigerian importers export their goods from Europe because of their open-door trade policy and low custom duties. The Nigerian importers will then resmuggle the goods back to Nigeria by road, paying customs officers, immigration officers, police officers, and others along the road. What a loss to the nation's economy!

She wore native attire to the office as if that is what is expected of Nigerians to wear. But the bad news is that she didn't realize that 99 percent of the materials used in making the clothes she wore was smuggled into the country. One would have thought that she should have revived the textile mill company in her backyard, the Asaba Textile Mill, which went under during the bad economic crisis caused by her boss. She supported trade embargo but privately enjoyed the ones smuggled in by die-hard importers who risk their lives and money to smuggle these goods into the country. Smuggled goods are bought by everybody no matter his or her class either for personal use or for re-selling them. These are the type of Nigerians Major Chukwuma called "Those that make the country look big for nothing before the international circles, those that corrupted our society and put the Nigerian political calendar backwards by their words and deeds."

President Obasanjo Sales of the People's Prime Real Estates and Corporations

Obasanjo once again demonstrated to Nigerians the stuff he is made of, that he can do anything he chooses to do at any time he wants to do it regardless of how Nigerians may feel because he thinks that nobody will ever hold him accountable, and perhaps he thinks that he is above the law and that Nigerians are fools and don't care what he does at the dead of the night.

Now he has found a newly minted friend, his finance minister, Ngozi, They have conspired to deprive Nigerians of their most expensive landed properties in the nation's most prime real estates, corporations, and oil wells without reforms. Obasanjo, as a military head of state, seized so many foreign businesses in Nigeria and gave them to his family, friends, cronies, and some dubious foreign businessmen and businesswomen operating in the country. As a military head of state, he seized banks such as former Standard Bank (now called First Bank), Barclays Bank (now called Union Bank), the UBA Bank, American Insurance Company, Federal Reinsurance Company, electricity corporation, oil refinery, and so on and passed them over to his favorites.

The federal government of Nigeria continued to pump money into these pits called banks because they cannot operate without the support of the rogue government of Nigeria. The federal government kept these banks alive because individual top government officials used them as a conduit pipe to siphon their ill-gotten wealth to their foreign banks' private accounts. These banks engage in money laundering to survive. One would have thought that Ngozi Iweala should have disengaged the federal government from owning and running commercial banks. Instead she became the biggest supporter of government ownership of commercial banks. She too had begun to pump billions of dollars into these pits called the nation's big banks, money that was never repaid. These banks will give loans to Nigeria's rich crooks who will never repay it or use it to create jobs. Instead they claim to be billionaires while the masses suffer. Most banks in the country engage in money laundering in order to stay afloat; without which they will never survive for a day in Nigeria's current economy.

You could remember the day the government seized Bank of America. It was a night in the daytime, a very sad day for the country and its economy. The question one should ask is, Was this done as a result of lack of common sense and shortsightedness? The banks they had already seized are not performing well, and why are they repeating the same mistake over and over again? One would guess that the reasons may be lack of logic or just wickedness. They renamed Bank of America and called it Savannah Bank. They named those they wanted to be the managers of this seized bank, and after milking the bank dry, they abandoned it. The government will now shop for another obscure buyer with little money but with big titles across names, and the bank is handed over to him or her, and after two or three years, the bank is folded. The government will toss the bank to another willing purchaser. This time around it was tossed into the hands of a former state governor, who was the last purchaser of Bank of America before the bank finally ended its existence in Nigeria.

The government of course knew that it will be impossible for a Nigerian buyer to own and manage one of the world's largest banks.

After the buyer collects whatever money that was left in the bank, then a notice of Out of Business will be placed on the bank doors. That was how Bank of America ended its existence in Nigeria.

Wonders never end in Nigeria. Military decrees inflicted the worst economic, social, and political mayhem to this nation that anyone would wonder why this happened. Did they ever realize the economic and social consequences of their actions? Is their purpose a sort of set ideas to do great things for the nation but it backfired? Why did they attack Western investments? Were they just completely naïve? The first rejection of Western investment took place towards the end of the nineteenth century, but why repeat it again in the twenty-first century when the world has teamed up together in the name of global economy and global world? No lesson was learnt.

My Reaction on Privatizations

When Obasanjo was given a second chance instead of him to use it as an opportunity to reverse himself from his previous use of military decrees to downgrade the economy, he jumped in to do the same thing over and over again. He was expected to undo his previous military style economic decrees by mustering the courage to return the businesses he seized years ago to their foreign owners instead of selling them to Nigerians. He was also expected to start top-to-bottom reforms before embarking on the use of another destructive economic policy. He failed to grab the opportunity but instead embarked into another round of destructive economic and social policy that only favors the rich.

But Nigerians have rested their hope on his finance minister, Okonjo-Iweala, to assist him by offering him sound economic advice on how to adopt a new economic pattern, but she failed to do so.

She should have advised him on how to return the country's failed economy to a healthy working economy.

I admired her achievement at the World Bank, which I think was basically the reason the president hired her. I was full of high hopes that she will help her boss to stop crashing the economy more and more, but that never happened, but instead she helped him to crash it more, leaving Nigerians without jobs and empty hopes for more than thirty years now. Every Nigerian, just like me, was disappointed when it was found out that she was always in full support of the president's economic policies whether helpful to the people of Nigeria or not. She should have told her boss, "Sir, before we embark on another destructive economic policy, we must do the first and most important thing, that is to embark on reforms. We cannot continue to put a round peg in a round hole and expect a better result."

Because of the new round of failures, Nigerians, it is time for change! It is a time for reforms, reforms, and reforms! The number one issue is that the federal government is too big and too large for nothing that does not affect the lives of the citizens and should be downsized. Secondly, the military leaders created thirty-six unsustainable tribal states that are solely dependent on federal government funding for existence, thousands of unsustainable family local governments that are also dependent on the federal government for funding and existence, hundreds of ministries and palatals all at the back of the federal government, high schools, higher institution of learning, the police, civil defense, federal road safety, federal board of examinations, sixty-six nonperforming federal research institutes that constitute only waste. Everything that moves in Nigeria is included in the federal budget, which are completely wasteful expenditures done by the federal government. After which nothing is left for capital project investment that will create decent jobs for the people. It created the biggest amount of upper and lower class white-collar and blue-collar crimes in the country. These are just few examples of how the federal government spends and wastes the people's oil revenue that I just listed. These are some of the reasons why major development is difficult to achieve in Nigeria. Having the World Bank presidential aide on board increases my hope for reforms, but nothing has happened. One would have thought that she would have found a better approach to revamp the economy with her boss.

The Sale of Nigeria's Most Priced Real Estates to the 1 percent Rich Nigerians

After the sale of the National Power Authority, the supply of power to Nigerians became worse. Power supply has become endemic forever, and the country is still experiencing fuel shortages. Does it mean that there is nobody in the country with enough common sense to propose dividing the power supply responsibilities to the states and let them decide the best way to deal with the matter? Nigerians continue to pay trillions and trillions of naira in electric bills every month for power supply they never get. This to me is unacceptable because all these monies go into individual private bank accounts. You may ask, What effort has President Jonathan put forward in revising all these dubious transactions that are working against the masses? He forgot that these illegal transactions are criminal acts committed against Nigerians by his predecessors. Nigeria is too big to be managed by one national power supply company. Every prime real estate owned by Nigerian people all over the country worth trillions and trillions of naira was sold by Obasanjo and his finance minister for peanuts to their families and friends or even foreigners who bought them through the use of surrogates. These properties must be probed and returned back to Nigerians. Today in Nigeria, every nook and corner of the country is mounted with generators by those who can afford it, regardless that it pollutes the air and not minding that it costs the economy billions of dollars every month. The presidential palace is also lighted with generators, and you would think that this will be an enough reason for the president to take action to provide nonstop electricity in the nation.

President Musa Umaru Yar'dua 2007-2010

Many Nigerians believed that Yar'dua did not want to join the presidential race but was cajoled by president Obasanjo to join the race because of the sitting president plan to crown the Yar'dua by hook or by crook. The 2007 presidential election was a sham and a fraud against Nigerians committed by president Obasanjo and his federal electoral commissioner Humphry Nwosu. Millions of Nigerians were denied their franchises to vote to elect a president of their choice. The election was marred with reports of vote rigging or polling agents not showing up at all at thousands of polling station across the country. I knew about this voting controversy because I was in Nigeria in 2007 on the day of the election. I had accompied my family and friends to the polling station on getting there was no sign to show that a presidential election was in effect because there was no polling agents and their ballot boxes were nowhere to be found.. Millions of Nigerians stood outside in the sun for hours to excise their franchises but no official showed up till voting ended and no one cares. I drove around the town the situation were the same all over which confirms that poll officials are not showing up to take votes. In fact, millions of voters in the former Eastern region, some parts of Delta state and many prominent citizens of these states were denied their franchise to vote. The nation's T.VS and Radio stations were overwhelmed with calls from disfranchised Nigerians to vent their anger and disappointments over the evil conduct of the election. The election fraud was well documented and the authorities heard it loud and clear that millions of Nigerians did not vote.

As an eye witness to the election fraud I called the American consulate in Lagos to report electoral fraud against Nigerian citizens. Because it was a weekend I spoke to Marine officer post one to register the frustrations and anger of millions of Nigerians who were denied their rights to vote. The officer promised to convey my message to the ambassador.

Every member of the ruling political party who ran for election or re-elections were rigged into power against the will of the people. Nigerians were very surprised when a sniveling cowardly, Humphrey Nwosu, the federal electoral commissioner called the stolen election for Yar'dua The actions, deeds and the performance of Yar'dua during his time in office demonstrated that he was an unwilling to serve as president. It is so sad that the country is governed by despots who do not respect democracy and the people are powerless to challenge the evil doers. The 2007 election should be probe and those who committed this electoral fraud should be held accountable.

It is time for the country change the federal electoral system. The system where a president appoints a federal electoral commissioner who become so powerful that he can do and undo as he wishes with the election results. He takes command and dances to the tune of the man or woman who appointed him. In future all board of elections commission should be the responsivities of the states and local government electoral boards who will conduct every election in the nation.

Proposed National Conference 2014

I was one of those Nigerians who were against the staging of a useless idea called national conference. My reasons for rejection are legions:

a. It was another dubious idea floated by the government to steal more than two billion naira budget for the conference.
b. The conference will be attended by only the 1 percent rich Nigerians that will never bring forth any new ideas or new innovations other than the tired old ideas we have heard for years.
c. Why national conference? We have the three branches of government who are paid billions and billions of naira to deal with these issues, which will be tabled at the conference. The nation has a constitutional assembly that will debate the issues and pass it into law without further waste of scarce resources.
d. Why not call for referendum that will allow Nigerian citizens the opportunity to express their opinions on the issues regarding their future and the future of the nation? Why not the president and the lawmakers organize town-hall meetings to sell their ideas to the people instead of the use of concentrated opinion that will rob the people their opinions and waste billions of naira? What happened in using scientific polling to gather the people's opinion?
e. Before the conference began, delegates to the conference have been grouped into tribal representatives that do not reflect the true Nigerian national character.
f. While the government plans to squander two billion naira on the national conference, Nigerian higher institutions of learning have locked their students out of the classroom for almost more than a year because of lack of funding

by the government. These children are supposed to be the nation's future leaders, but we watch as their future is turned upside down on a daily basis. The educational system in the country is in complete disarray because of lack of funding, lack of trained teachers, and mismanagement plus incompetence. It is a shame that this government will overlook all these problems and embark in a spending spree that will cost the nation huge amounts of money to please the rich and distract Nigerians from the serious problems facing the nation such as: the health care system, the power supply system, roads, the water system, the educational system, the national security, and so many more.

Unemployment in the country is one of the worst in the world. Life in Nigeria is based on survival of the fittest, dog-eat-dog kind of existence. Many Nigerians fleeing the country in droves in order to escape poverty and unemployment and some die on their way out. And it is very sad. Yet the government still has the nerve to waste this huge amount of money for another worthless gathering. Many Nigerians have known that the highest achievement that will come out of this conference will be the long introduction of delegates attending the conference, which goes like this, "His Excellency, Honorable, president, governor, senator, representative, doctor, professor, chief, barrister, engineer, architect, alhaji, alhaja, Mrs., lady, dame, chatered accountant, reverend, and bishop." This is the way a couple will be introduced to the conference attendees. It is all title mania conference, an ostentatious display of one's importance and ill-gotten wealth. The conference will end in nothing but all sounds and no fury as usual.

What Nigerians needs and want are jobs, jobs, jobs, free public education, clean tap water in every home, free public health care system with quality doctors and nurses in clean environments, quality food items (not cassava bread) as promised by the finance minister, twenty-four hours nonstop electricity supply, good roads to facilitate the movement of people and goods, peace and harmony with one another, a government of accountability. They also want their civil rights to be protected, a government that will wisely use the people's resources to create a better life and opportunities for everyone in the country, and a government that is based on honesty, decency, and integrity. Nigerians want patriotic men and women, those Nigerians who passionately love and care for their country as well as those Nigerians who are not tainted with bribery and corruption and have no atom of tribalism, nepotism, and favoritisms in their mind to fix the country. They want visionary leaders that understand where the shoe pinches. They want men and women filled with wisdom, knowledge, and understanding and not those with their showmanship paper qualifications who are criminals. It is time for political socialization in the country. It is time to uproot, destroy, and rebuild, rebuild greater, stronger, and better.

Is Nigeria a Lawless Nation?

Yes, Nigeria can be described as a lawless nation, not because there are no laws and statutes. There are plenty of it from the federal government to state governments and local governments, but they remain buried by the authorities to facilitate their commission of economic crimes against their people. The laws in Nigeria are made by the superiors for the inferiors to obey, hence everyone is a law onto his or herself in the nation.

Think of it, in a nation where members of the executive branch of the government, the national state assembly members, local government officials break the laws they made, who then will obey the law? The law is broken with impunity so as to enable them to unlawfully enrich themselves at the expense of the masses. A nation where every street and highway are amounted with roadblocks by all types of uniformed men and women employed in the security forces, starting from the police force, mobile police forces, military forces, customs, immigration, road safety agent, traffic wardens, just to mention a few. You would think that they are out there to protect the country and its citizens, but they are out there only to collect bribes.

Every commercial vehicle and noncommercial vehicle that approaches any of these roadblocks are forced to pay bribe money before access is allowed. They also confiscate goods with an excuse that it is contraband. These roadblocks have also resulted to so many vehicle accidents that have sent so many Nigerians to their untimely deaths without the government raising an eyebrow nor has anyone been held accountable because the lives of Nigerians masses and their property are not important and therefore not protected under the law.

Fuel tanks have exploded when unknowingly running into these roadblocks, which as today continue to cause so many collateral damages when innocent Nigerians' lives end untimely because these roadblocks mount to collect illegal bribes from innocent citizens. At the same time these officers always flee their roadblock posts upon sighting the bad guys. These officers abuse their power and fail to uphold the law they are hired to uphold. In fact, the people live in a police state in a democratic nation.

The 1999, 2007, and 2011 Elections

In the 1999, 2007, and 2011 elections, many well-known criminals like drug pushers and international scam artists, and embezzlers were gathered and rigged into power where they continue with their immoral lifestyles because no one cares about the law.

It is a nation where a state governor or state governors can short down an entire local government and sack its elected officials. Officials that were elected like them are driven out of office. The governor or governors succeeded because the nation's executive branch and the judicial branch do not care whether a law is broken or not. Throughout the governor's duration in the office, the elected officials were never allowed to return—anarchy, if you will.

It is a nation where a government minister could spend 225 million naira to purchase an armored car for herself with the people's money and the executive branch and the congress will not raise an eyebrow. Don't ask, don't tell. The law is made by the superior for the inferior to obey.

A nation where two-way traffic lanes will be turned into five to eight lanes of traffic, resulting in heavy traffic that keeps motorists waiting in traffic for six to twelve hours because nobody obeys the law.

It is a nation where the landlords are the kings. They demand two to three years' rent in advance and then demand extra illegal money called the landlord kola nut fees, landlords' association fees, and attorney fees and agent fees that the landlord and his gang dishonestly skim from a prospective tenant after collecting three years' rent is paid in advance. Here it means that the future tenant has been deprived for at least another two years' rent not accounted in the rent already paid. It is just another illegal money landlords, his attorney, and his agent collect from a new tenant. It is mandatory because if you don't pay the illegal fees, you cannot find a place to live.

This crime is imitated and committed by some Nigerian lawyers who cannot find a better job. Instead of these lawyers obeying and interpreting the rent laws, they become the major breakers of the law. The rent laws are disregarded by the attorneys and the landlords they represent in order to dupe their fellow citizens, many of whom don't have a job or visible means of livelihood. They encourage crimes when they ask jobless citizens to pay such a huge amount of money for rent.

This is a nation where illiterate, untrained auxiliary nurses are permitted to administer medications, give injections, deliver babies, and are preferred by Nigerian quack doctors above Nigerian registered nurses because they are cheap to hire, therefore jeopardizing the lives of unsuspecting patients. Some of these auxiliary nurses owns drugstores and use them to prescribe injections and medications to patients who do not know that these fakes are not qualified and not legally permitted to handle drugs, something that has caused so many deaths.

These uneducated, untrained auxiliary nurses are hired by the government to head community health care centers above doctors and qualified registered nurses. Also, the Nigerian environmental officers have hijacked the nursing profession duties instead of environmental duties. I guess they have no job assignments in their fields.

It is a nation where pharmacists sell their licenses to unqualified, unlicensed drugstore owners to cover them to commit medical atrocities.

It is a nation where second-year medical students have already started operating illegal clinics openly while some general medical practitioners become surgeons without a surgeon's license and illegally operate on patients who may need or may not need a surgery. These unlicensed medical surgeons conduct this illegal surgery because it pays them more financially. For years the nation's health care system has been under assault because nobody obeys the laws.

It is a nation where members of uniformed security forces could beat their fellow citizens to purple or even to death and nobody raises an eyebrow. Instead of protecting the citizens they are paid to protect, they abuse them and break the laws they are supposed to uphold with reckless abandon.

It is needless to discuss about those men and women who claim to be the nation's lawmakers because they are the highest lawbreakers. The laws they pass and are supposed to obey and uphold, they break it with impunity.

It is a nation where leaders at all levels often walk away scot-free after they are caught breaking the laws and are given a slap on the wrist, and cases are closed even if he or she was caught committing the most heinous crime.

This is a nation where public policies are based on rumors and superstition.

This is a nation where every public policy is quickly converted into bribery and corruption and turned into a fraud industry. These are just few examples of how public policy once enacted becomes bribery and corruption and ends up as fraud industries

This can be said to be the mother of all lawlessness in this country when law enforcement official gave express pass to commercial vehicles to take over a federal four lanes highway stretching from Coconut bus stop to Tin Can Island seaport and all the way to Apapa seaports was turn into parking lots year after years after they collect bribes from transporters. This highway lead to the two most important seaports in the nation. This road is blocked side by side, center and front with oil tankers, heavy haulage trunks and all manner of trucks with serious emission problems. This road is under seize to the extent that workers cannot drive to work, public transport cannot take workers and business people to work, even pedestrians cannot walk to work except to snake around the road to walk between five to ten miles to work and business while they absorb all manners of dust and heat. After seeing this horrendous act been penetrated on a nation's highway, a gateway to the nation's commercial nerve center you just felt sorry for this country because it doesn't understand the meaning of economy. You can imagine the trillions of naira this country loses every year because of this senseless melancholy. Your first reactions is to ask yourself if any government does exist in this country and how about law enforcement agents does they exist? It a death trap and who cares? Again, from mile 2 to Okokomako every side of the road are clogged with all manners of oil tankers and heavy commercial trucks from right to left snarling traffic for hours on end which is a huge loss of manpower, another death traps. It's even funnier that you will find law enforcement officials place in charge to control traffic and prevent vehicles clogging on these road collecting bribes, drinking beer, smoking cigarettes, enjoying pepper soup and chasing women I witnessed this activities myself. It is so sad that private transport owners will have the nerve to convert a federal highway into their private parking lots under the nose of the government and the law enforcement officials because of bribery and corruptions. Oviously, there is no government in this country? You may ask when will ethic and morals be restore in this country. I do not know how and where the messes in this country will begin its clean up to make it a better society. Every law enforcement officials ever served in these locations must be fired. You wonder if they are journalists in this country.

The solution to this problem is for the federal government to fine the states and local governments one million naira for each vehicle found idly parked on federal highways blocking the free flow of traffic from all directions. The states and local government could as well fine the owners of these vehicles one million naira for each vehicle found idly parked on the highways even if it is a break dawn. The government should enact a law that will mandate all oil tankers and other commercial vehicles to operate only from 10:00 pm to 6:00 am from Monday to Friday. They must be off the road by 6:00 am and resume again from 10:00 pm to 6:00 am no exceptions. This nation must learn how to enforce the law for the safety her citizens

Obasanjo's Import Ban, 1976

Since 1976, which is almost thirty-nine years ago, the military government of General Obasanjo banned the importation of goods with military decrees even though the nation does not produce a pin of its own. After the ban, young men and women took to smuggling. They smuggled into the country all kinds of banned goods. They did not stop there. They were able to smuggle in containers loaded with drugs from Latin America and containers loaded with fake currencies of both local and international currencies, which are smuggled into the country through Nigerian seaports, airports, and through the borders of the nation's neighboring countries on a daily basis, and they are quickly given a passages by the members of the Nigerian customs department and other law enforcement agencies with the active knowledge and support of Nigerian top officials.

The federal government loses billions and billions of US dollars' worth of import duties and other port levies to smart Nigerian smugglers because of the government's antiquated international trade laws. Without this smuggling, the nation's economy would have collapsed completely. The money to be collected as government revenues now go into the private pockets of Nigerian customs officers and Nigerian top governmental officials and some smart Nigerian businessmen and businesswomen on a monthly and yearly basis.

These days Nigerian importers use the seaports of neighboring African countries where there are no trade barriers or unfriendly import laws to import their goods and pays billions of dollars of customs duties to these countries and then turn around to resmuggle these goods back into Nigeria through the nation's common borders. While the government of these nations collect billions of dollars of import duty from Nigerian smugglers because of their relaxed import and export laws, the Nigerian government loses billions of dollars because they fixate their eyes on oil revenue. The smugglers get to the Nigerian side of the border then have to pay bribes to Nigerian customs and other Nigerian security forces to give them access to smuggle in their goods. This goes to show that the Nigerian side of the border is not secure.

In this scenario among these nations, which of them can be said to economically smarter and wiser?

Is it the Nigerian government with its antiquated trade embargo laws that are harming its economy or the governments of its neighboring countries that have free trade laws that attract Nigerian smugglers to do business in their countries? No matter what type of trade laws is made by government they always turn out to be counterproductive.

Do you blame these brave Nigerian smugglers who are helping to prevent the country from imminent economic collapse, or do you blame Nigerian law enforcement officials who collect government revenues as their own? All the blame must be placed on the doorstep of antiquated economic policies and the government not weighing its effects and consequences on the people's means of livelihood. Though the Nigerian leaders banned these goods from coming into the country, they too smuggle the same goods into the country for their personal use. They are champions in breaking the law they made.

Reforms

These bank aided and abetted those who stole government funds, drug pushers and the 419ers to hide their ill-gotten wealth. Tell me, in a nation where banks do not offer credit and loans to individuals and business owners, how then do these banks generate profit in order to stay in business?

It is only reforms that can save the Nigerian banking industry, and should start from banks from the Central Bank of Nigeria to all the commercial banks in the country should face a serious audit, investigation, and probe because it will help the government to reform the banking system. The Central Bank only should be audited going back to fifty years. Over 95 percent of these banks will go under if audited. Nigerians deserve a better banking system that will lift up the economy. The banking industry has not helped to grow the nation's economy, instead they rip it off.

Education, government jobs, Jamb, WAEC, National Youth Service and Housing are public services where poor families are often subjected to extreme demands of bribes by government officials that should face serious reforms. Its reforms will be detailed inside the paper.

It was fraud and mismanagement that ended the National Provident Fund, a program that was similar to the United States Social Security Program and was never probed. This too will be reformed and restarted again

It was fraud and mismanagement and crisis that ended the National Identity Program that was supposed to ID all Nigerians and everyone that calls the country a home. This will go through reforms to make better because it is needed and very important.

A nation without a well-written, articulated constitution will not rise to greatness. The constitution (the supreme law of the land) should be revisited, either to write a new one or to add amendments to the currently existing one, because it is the nation's foundation. A new constitution that will serve as a road map to peace, unity, and to end all forms of discrimination in the country should be considered.

As recently as this year, December 2013, when I was about to file a lawsuit in a state high court, I was advised by many people not to do it because there is no justice in the nation's court system because it is only the VIPs who can obtain justice against the plaintiffs.

They told me that it is a waste of time, that I should not do it. They told me that it is the amount of money one has that will determine who wins a case. However, I rejected their opinion and filed the lawsuit. Even though the defendant never showed up in court to defend himself, he won the case. The case was about shipping fraud.

Reforms can make some of these high-court judges stand for elections in order to become judges. The criminal justice system should be reformed.

Political Socialization

Reform platforms should be used to determine the way to change guard and hand over the rein of government to the next generations of Nigerians. The old political disorders should come to an end, and a brand-new country will be started. The youths are free to demand for political socialization and transfer of power from old politicians who have consistently failed their nation for more than half a century by misleading and mismanaging the nation's resources

Those men and women who Major Chukwuma mentioned when he said, "Our enemies are the profiteers, the swindlers, and the men in high and low places that seek bribes and demand 10 percent, those that seek to keep the country divided permanently so that they can remain in office as ministers or VIPs," should be sacked from politics.

American Constitution

I have come to love the American constitution. I have nothing but praise for the framers of this masterpiece of a document called the American constitution (the supreme law of the land) put together by the founding fathers that went far beyond what America will be on the day of the constitution convention but also on what America will be in generations and generations to come. In their quest for a better America and better world, they hammered out a document that has made America the richest and the greatest country in world. "We hold these truths to be self-evident that all men are created equal" (Congress, July 4, 1776).

It was due to the hard work of visionary, disciplined, passionate American men as well as dreamers, innovators, and thinkers who, with their wisdom, were divinely inspired to lay down the greatest foundation of the American constitution on top of a rock that has made America the greatest country in the world and has withstood the test of time. America is respected, loved, hated, and feared by friends and foes around the world because of the constitution that stood for freedom for all. The founding fathers did not close the book but instead left it open for interpretations and amendments for generations of Americans. It is even more amazing that moving and nonmoving things, breathing and nonbreathing things are protected under the constitution. It amazes me to watch generation after generation of Americans continue to build on this foundation called the American constitution, never letting it down.

Can you imagine what America could have been in a nation of diversities without this constitution?

African-American

If anyone is to ignore the contributions of African-Americans in American history and its greatness and wealth I think that person is an enemy. They travelled a long and tedious journey, but I am glad that they made it, thanks to the American constitution. I always admire their guts and their achievements that they made in a very short period of time. They deserve a pat on their backs. It wasn't an easy achievement.

Nigerians in particular and Africans in general should take a cue from how African-Americans worked themselves up to the top in America and had become a force to be reckoned with in the world. Nigeria in particular should ally with African-American professionals in all fields of human endeavor to help the country to rebuild their failed state.

It is time for African nations to get up and walk the walk and run the run to reverse the misfortune of their various nations.

I salute Frederick Douglass, Martin Luther King Jr., and all the great African-African men and women who, through their efforts, voice, and handiwork, fought to make all Americans equal under the law and to end separations of people in schools and public places because they believe in the American constitution. Yet many more work remains to be done.

It is about time the African nations stop ignoring the potentials in African-Americans if their quest is to attract American investors. Africans should stop now and embrace them because they are forces to be reckoned with in America.

As Nigeria in particular and African nations in general struggle to find their economic relevance at home and at the world stage, they should look up to the African-American professionals as mentors.

The time has come when African leaders will come to America in search of investment opportunities and will first not knock at the doors of the African-American professional who are their brothers and sisters who will be willing to assist in arranging high-powered meetings with American investors that are interested in investing in Nigeria and other African nations.

The time will come when African leaders will begin to build trust with their African-American counterparts. The crisis in Africa calls for external help. In case the African leaders can be manly enough to admit their failures and are ready to seek for help, it will argue well for the continent. Nigeria in particular and African nations in general should open up a friendship dialogue with African-Americans in the United States. An international organization should be formed between the brothers and sisters to share common future goals, an organization that will join these brothers and sisters together.

Honorary African Citizenship for African-Americans

It could be seen as a good intentions if interested African countries to grant African-Americans honorary citizenships. This wonderful gesture, I guess, will give them the opportunity to enter African countries as honorary African citizens without visas. With their American passport, they can travel to any African country and enter as honorary citizens for business or as a tourist. This, I believe, will be a good economy sense for African nations. The African-Americans' buying power is about 1.1 trillion dollars a year in the US economy, which is bigger than the entire African continent's annual budget. Nigeria in particular and African nations in general can no longer afford to ignore this demographic. This is an idea Nigeria in particular and African nations in general should embrace because it will be good for them.

Also, American business investors, whether black or white, that are interested in investing in Nigeria should be granted honorary citizenship to facilitate their entry into the country. These potential investors should be free to bring in their supporting staffs and should as well be granted automatic residency so they should not be tied down with immigration bureaucracy.

The Nigerian government in particular and African nations should make laws to protect all foreign investments from being seized by African despots. Security must be a top priority throughout African nations in order to allay the fears of potential investors, who may harbor doubts about their personal safety and their investments.

The world has become a global village, and Nigeria should take advantage of it to build a rainbow nation where all tribes, languages, cultures, religious beliefs, blacks, reds, and whites will one day live side by side with one another, and the people and the nation will benefit from the pools of talent, skill, and creativity from men and women of all walks of life who will call the nation their country.

No matter what, Nigeria will need the help of American technological experts in the future if the nation's leaders are serious about fixing the failed state. The future goals of the nation are to be part the twenty-first-century global world economy of nations. The nation's primary goals should be gaining the latest technologies in the world.

My use of the American constitution is to show for example how a nation can achieve greatness, economic prosperity, and efficiency by having written laws that work. A nation where its core principles are upheld, respected, and maintained will prosper. America is a nation where its constitutional amendments protect everyone's rights.

The 1914 Amalgamation of Nigeria by British Colonists and the Creation of Thirty-Six States

Frederick Lugard, the colonial administrator of the then British protectorates of Northern and Southern Nigeria, amalgamated both. They were divided into three regions namely the northern region, the eastern region, and the western region. They existed together through the time of Nigeria's attainment of independence from Britain in October 1, 1960.

For a long period of time, many Nigerians seemed to be blaming the British colonial masters for their policy of bringing people of different cultures and religious beliefs together as one nation. Many theorize that the colonial masters used deliberate conspiracies to punish Nigerians by bringing these three beds of strange fellows together so they could remain enemies forever.

The question is whether the amalgamation was a good or bad idea. I intend to believe that the colonial masters did this with the best intentions for Nigerians. The original intention for amalgamation was to create big states with big cities, suburbs, counties. This is a big country that has the advantages of becoming a rich and prosperous nation. The issue is to determine whether it was done on the basis of creating a big, diversified country that will bring together a large pool of lands, large population, and natural resources, which in addition will bring together men and women that will live cooperatively side by side with each other and apply their human potentials and natural resources to build a great nation that will benefit everyone in the nation. But instead the nation's leaders blew the opportunities into thin air by using tribalism to divide and conquer.

I do not believe that the purpose of creating the three regions was to divide the country into tribal states but rather for the purpose of diversity. If you look at the three original regions, you can see that it was diversified to the point that different tribes where included in each region to live and grow together. However, because those Nigerians who held the power then were so blinded with tribalism and the seeking of political patronage, they recklessly blew up the opportunity and turned around to create thirty-six unsustainable tribal states and blamed the colonial masters for their failures. If these leaders had visions, they would have used the opportunity of the three big regions to build a strong, united, prosperous nation for all. The idea behind the creation of the three regions by the colonial masters was misunderstood by the Nigerian leaders. Absolutely, there was no reason whatsoever for them to embark on the destructiveness of creating thirty-six unsustainable tribal states that are contributing to the biggest problems and undermine the development of the nation, which successfully helped to make the country a tribalized nation.

Western Nigerian Premier Election, 1960

Not until after independence and after the colonial masters left did the newly minted Nigerian politicians begin to use tribal lineage to divide and conquer to win political favors from their kindred. Many Nigerians will still remember quite vividly what happened in the western region between Awolowo and Azikiwe before the civil war after the first postindependence premier election there. That election can be said to have started the first sign of Nigerian tribal war that will later engulf the whole country to a point of no return, which became part of the reasons for the civil war and the current biggest nightmare for the nation thus so far.

When Dr. Azikiwe won the premiership of the western region over Awolowo, though the westerners voted for Azikiwe, Awolowo rejected the election by saying that Azikiwe is not a Yoruba man but an Igbo man and sent Azikiwe racing back to the east, where he came from, to contest the premiership in the eastern region. The dreams of Azikiwe about one united country was defeated by Awolowo's actions after Azikiwe won the western Nigerian premiership elections.

After Awolowo sacked the winner of the election, he took over as the premier of Western Nigerian above a fellow Nigerian who was officially elected by the people. Owning to this, the stage for tribalism and corruption has been set at the very beginning after the nation gained independence. From thence the spread of tribal consciousness all over the nation began to take shape and never looked back up to these days. However, tribalism became more pronounced during and after the Nigerian Civil War. The nation became so tribally divided that even their public policies are based on tribal patronage.

Nigeria's First Three Regions

Because of the Nigerian political class failure to articulate the silver lining on the amalgamation of the northern and the southern protectorates, they failed to recognize the benefits of the amalgamation. They failed to capitalize on the ideas of three big regions that would have been renamed states and carve out cities and counties that would have helped the nation to expand and prosper.

Remember that the colonial masters led and managed the three regions from 1914 to 1960 successfully without problems until the country was granted independence on October 1, 1960, when things began to fall apart. Also, the fight for independence was fought on the platforms of the three regions. Why then after independence, instead of a united nation, the Nigerian leaders chose division instead of unity? This division in the nation has resulted to lack of peace, lack of cooperation, leading to underdevelopments because incompetent men and women are favored to run the country while those who are well equipped to run the country became onlookers or may not even have jobs.

The colonial masters' idea of amalgamation was first and foremost, I guess, was for administrative purposes to make it easier to manage and to help lay down a solid foundation in the preparation for the future of Nigeria as a big country with big population and boundless resources that were set to make Nigeria a great nation. Had Nigerian leaders taken advantage of the diversities of the amalgamation, the nation would have been very competitive with large pools of talented, skilled, and creative citizens. At which time everyone will benefit regardless of what tribe you are.

Had it been that the three regions were carved into cities, suburbs, and counties, it would have helped to bridge the gap of tribalism in our society, and every Nigerian, not matter where they live in any part of the nation, will be classified as citizens and not as nonindigene, as is happening today. The failure of our national and local leaders to consider the benefit of a diversified nation was an unpardonable crime. Due to lack of foresight and tribalism, they created thirty-six unsustainable tribal states that can be pinned to be the cause of underdevelopment, poverty, unemployment, disease, and hunger everywhere in the nation today.

Placing tribalism above the future of the nation has indeed robbed the nation of its potentials from all walks of life, hence it has become the major cause of mismanagement and corruptions in the nation. Tribalism, nepotism, favoritism, bribery and corruptions are the primary reasons why incompetence gain the advantage to rule the country. Amalgamation was a good omen for the nation but was misunderstood and squandered by Nigerian leaders. It would have helped to hold Nigeria together while making it a great nation. The Nigerian leaders failed to take advantage of the forces of diversities where no citizen will be judged on the basis of the content of his tribe but on the content of his character. The failure to grab this opportunity robbed Nigerians of the chance to build a just and a progressive, peaceful, united country.

Tribalism remains one of the primary reasons why all the powers of government appear concentrated at the federal levels, reducing the states and local government to nothing but a shadow only allowed to wait for handouts from the federal government before they could function.

The Nigerian postindependence national and local leaders failed woefully to see the silver lining in the nation's three regions that would have been a road map to become the African giant and the greatest and richest country in Africa if tribalism had not overclouded their sense of reason.

Of course, it is still not yet too late to reverse the course if the country is ready to harness its human capital, the natural resources, and all the beautiful and good people in the country and the world to build a great nation. Nation development begins from the grass-roots, not from the top of the mountain. The duty of the federal government is to fund projects, regulate and make laws. But grass-roots developments should be responsible for states cities, boroughs, counties, and suburbs. States and local government must be capable of generating at least 80 percent of their annual revenues and not solely rely on the federal government.

Tribalism remains the biggest problem that reared its ugly head after the nation attained independence and was one of the biggest reasons Nigerians fought the civil war. And up to this moment, the problem remains and has gotten worse, and no government has made an effort to address it, not talk less of finding solutions to end it as the nation knows it. The government's failure to take concrete actions to address one of the biggest problems undermines the united progressive development of the nation; it is a serious issue that must be tackled by Nigerians.

Undoing the Thirty-Six Unsustainable States

How could Nigerian leaders who created these unsustainable tribal states defend their actions? They tore the country into thirty-six unsustainable states and created additional thousands of tribal family local governments that cannot boost of any single infrastructure. Local governments like state governments depend upon the federal government handouts for their survival. The federal government allocates funds on a monthly basis to sustain these states and local governments; it looks insane.

The allocation funds to the states and local governments are used primarily for overhead cost only. After workers are paid, whatever money that is left are often stolen by officials. No money will be left to service public programs such as education, housing, health care, clean water, electricity, roads, welfare programs, or to secure the citizens. The states and the local governments generate little or no revenue of its own, and it must depend on the federal government to fund allocations that never benefit the poor masses by creating jobs and opportunities for them.

How to Recreate and Reduce the Thirty-Six Unsustainable Tribal States to Six or Seven States

The question that should be in everyone's lips is, What was the wisdom and vision behind the creation of thirty-six unsustainable tribal states and thousands of unsustainable local governments? Do you think these states' creators love this nation as to do this harm? These states cannot fund themselves but depend on the federal government for their existence, and for this reason, it undermines any effort ever made towards economic development, and that would have raised the standard of living for the people. The federal government is solely responsible for funding over 80 percent of the thirty-six states and thousands of local governments. The funds allocated are mainly used to pay overhead cost, and whatever is left is stolen. The evils underlining the creation of these many unsustainable tribal states were purely on the basis of politics, tribalism's favoritism, nepotism, and corruption. It wasn't meant to address the nation's underdevelopment or to benefit the masses but to benefit those politicians who will become governors, senators, representatives, ministers, commissioners, VIPS, and the 10 percenters.

Do you think that the military leaders and political leaders who divided their nation into thirty-six unsustainable tribal states were based on sound economic reasoning? These states have been created for more than thirty years, and none of them can boast or show any tangible economic progress of note. Those who were responsible in creating these states did not first consider how the states will survive financially. Trillions of naira are wasted on a daily basis to maintain states and local governments that work against the people instead of for the people. The states and local governments do not create jobs for the people. Their private sector economy is in a dump and doesn't exist.

The only beneficial are those that occupy the seat of power and their families and friends. The federal government allocations to states and the local government have never been used for the construction of critical infrastructures, creation of jobs, good education, health care, welfare, housing, water, and so many other programs for the poor. Development in Nigerian will not go anywhere unless and until a comprehensive reform takes place throughout the nation. These unsustainable states should be dismantled, leaving only six or seven of them to exist.

Reduce Thirty-Six States to Six or Seven States Only

Although I am not sure if any one will ever answer all these questions, it is time now to decide the best way for the nation to move forward and decide how to create six or seven new states to be called states of inclusiveness and sustainability for all Nigerians.

Nigeria has become a nation of separated tribal people but one country. It is so sad that a country can be so divided and expect anything good to come out of it. The nation is so blindly separated among tribes and dialects that it is difficult to call it a nation.

Ever since Nigerian leaders decided to divide Nigerian people into thirty-six unsustainable tribal states for their own political gains, the country has never been the same again. Today each state discriminates against their fellow Nigerians on state and local jobs and housing and even schools on basis of nonindigenes that have swept across the country. If you live in any of these thirty-six states for years or you are born in that state by parents who were not born in that state, you are not considered a citizen of that state or local government when it comes to employment, education, housing, and other state and local benefits, which will be denied to him or her on the basis of nonindigene status. These too must end.

Unlike America, there are no interest groups to file class-action lawsuits against offending states. Lawyers in the country have not done that coupled with the fact that in the country, people are not aware about their rights in the constitution.

The reason behind my advocacy for states of inclusiveness is because I want Nigeria to be a great country, but Nigeria cannot be a great country if they are tribally divided and scattered like sheep without a shepherd. I want Nigerian people to put their talents and skills together in order to build a just and a progressive society for all.

The proposal to create states and local governments of inclusiveness is to abolish the entire thirty-six tribal states and replace them with six or seven states that Nigerians of different tribes and dialects will be given a state, and they will to live together in one state as citizens. The Igbos, Yorubas, Hausas, and other dialects will be included in one new state to be created until six or seven states are carved out from the existing thirty-six states. No tribe in Nigeria will ever be given a state alone. Tribes must be joined together to be accepted as a state. Nowhere in the nation should the word *indigenes* or *nonindigenes* be used against a fellow citizen. If new states are created in the manner described above, this will surely bring peace, unity, and progress to the people of Nigeria.

A Look at How the New States Will Turn Out

For example, in hypothetical statement, a new state can be created to start from Anambra State, part of Delta State, part of Edo State, part of Kogi State, part of Kwara State through the federal capital Abuja and Kano or Kaduna and to be named Abuja State. Then a district will be carved out of Abuja State, which may be named, for example, say, Stone Mountain Districts of ABUJA (Dosma Rocky Mountain District of Abuja [RMDA]), that will operate independently from the federal government seat of power. Abuja State will be named the city as district of Stone Mountain. The district of Stone Mountain will be a city with its boroughs to cater for the residents of the new state with an elected major of the city, even a governor of the state, and its own police department, housing and urban development department (HUDD), health care department, board of education, board of elections and welfare department (HRA). The city will control Abuja land use. They will have their elected state assembly members, district council members. Inclusive states like the one mentioned above will be created throughout Nigeria until six or seven states are created with no tribal attachment or sentimental names used to create them. Let's say for example the newly created states' names will be like these: (1) Oaktree State, (2) Festac State, (3) Georgia State, (4) Rainbow State, (5) Sunset State, and (6) Sunshine State.

Reforming and downsizing the unsustainable, money-wasting thirty-six states will save the nation and the people trillions of naira and bring meaningful developments to the nation.

If twenty-nine or thirty states are eliminated, the nation will be aiming to achieve the progress of creating jobs and opportunities and as well as building modern states, cities, and suburbs for the people with the money saved from cutting down the states. When, say, twenty-nine or thirty states are taken off and just six or seven states are created to replace them, the trillions of naira saved can be used to start building critical infrastructures. The benefit of creating non-tribal states is huge because of its diversity and should be pursued. It will be an advantage for Nigerians because various ethnic groups and different religious beliefs and cultures will be able to live side by side with one another in one state or local government as stakeholders that will help to caution mistrust and end all tribally divided and hating one another and effort must be made by every citizen to help end the tribal segregation of Nigerians, which was the result when thirty-six unsustainable states was created. Nigerians must accept and celebrate diversities as blessings and not a curse. They must look out for the advantageousness of various tribes living and sharing one state with one another as their home. We must look for the advantageousness and not for its disadvantageousness.

Benefits of New States

The most beneficial and the most important good news about these new states are just too many that will last for centuries to come. The most immediate benefits are as follows:

1. States will have, cities, counties, boroughs, and suburbs that will be big enough to be able to be socially and economically sustainable. They will finance and run their governments without depending on the federal government for everything. They will be sustainable enough to build their own critical infrastructures in order to create jobs and run their education, health care department, police department, prisons, housing development, criminal justice system without waiting for the federal government's monthly handouts.

2. It will spur healthy and positive competition where potential talents will be recognized to help in developments. Both the new states and the federal government will save huge amounts of money as a result of these reforms.
3. Then this money saved will be used to create and build the critical infrastructures needed to move and stabilize the economy.
4. A very solid foundation for a unified nation, progress, and prosperity would have been laid for generations and generations of Nigerians to come as a basis for them to grow and prosper and will make them proud of their country and thankful to their forbears.
5. The country will be built stronger, bigger, and better for everyone.
6. The country will no longer be separated by tribes and dialects but will be united with love for one another and one common goal.
7. A big legacy is awaiting those who will take up this challenge to reform this country into a progressive nation.
8. A diversified states will be an advantage to everyone, the states will become competitive, whoever is interested in running for an elective office can do so where he lives, appointments to states and local offices will be a mix of different classes of Nigerians, states and local government jobs opportunity including benefits will be for those that need them. The use of state of origin to deny a fellow citizen his or her rights will no longer apply.
9. They will be better managed through grassroots developmental efforts.
10. States, cities, suburbs, counties will be empowered to make sure that its administration will directly affect and enrich the lives of their citizens. They also will have the

power to generate their own sources of revenues to run their own governments and create jobs, jobs, and jobs for their people and all Nigerians without much dependence on the federal government for about 90 percent of their revenues. They will be sustainable, and they will be able to source for 80 percent of their revenues while getting about 20 percent of funding from the federal government for education, health care, police department, fire services department, water development, road constructions, housing developments.

States, cities, counties, suburbs will be able to choose their own private power supply company that supply them nonstop electricity every day without additional cost to the government. In fact, both the local governments, state and federal, will gain through collecting taxes from the energy companies and the consumers. The judicial branches, the states executive branch, states assembly, the states, cities, suburbs, and counties judicial, city majors, states governors, and political appointees in every local government and states governments will reflect the national characters as it exists in the federal government today. Elections from national, states, cities, suburbs, and counties or any other type elections will be an open contest for Nigerians in any part of the country where they reside. No Nigerian will be forced to run back to their so-called state of origin in order to contest any election; that individual must do so wherever he or she lives. This will serve as the best way to deal with the issue of nation tribal politics and discriminations. The emphasis on reforms would be to build a strong, formidable, just, and prosperous nation for all.

Big cities with at least five boroughs should be carved out of each city with elected major as the head and elected borough presidents. The new city council will have the speaker of the city council. This new arrangement can be called the popular sovereignty, a government in which the people rule. A broader range of people of different Nigerian tribes will share power to govern themselves. Also, in federalism system of government, "The national government is assigned the delegated powers, the states kept the reserved powers. Powers shared or exercised by national and state governments are known as concurrent powers"(United States Constitution). "United we stand, divided we fall."

When people coexist to love one another and care for one another, the result will be unity, peace, and progress. The biggest benefit that will come out of this downsizing of the states is that it will save Nigerian people more than 60 percent of the federal government fund allocations to the states that are wasted and never benefit the people. It is money thrown into the pits by the way of fraud, embezzlements, and pick-pocketing done by those who are given the privilege to manage the people's resources but rather choose to abuse their powers. It must not be allowed to continue because Nigerians are suffering while their leaders and their families and cronies enjoy better life with the money looted from them. Nigerians, you must uproot, destroy, rebuild better, bigger, and stronger.

The Three Original Regions

There should be no doubts the embarking on downsizing the thirty-six states to six or seven states will be quite a challenging task to do, but it can be done if the nation is serious about building a progressive and prosperous country. The former three regions and former midwestern region can serve as an example because they were created on the basis of tribal inclusiveness and not on tribal divide, which is quite different from current thirty-six states that were purely created on basis of individual tribes or dialects representatives. In the three original states and later the midwestern states were all created on the basis of tribal and dialects inclusiveness; it was so diversified that it was aimed to join all the tribes and dialects as stakeholders in each of these regions.

The options open for federal government should be nothing but to undo the thirty-six states and then recreate six or seven new tribal-free and dialect-free inclusive states. Its outcome will result to bigger states and bigger cities, boroughs, suburbs, and counties that will be a sustainable enough as to be self-financing. Half of the money saved by eliminating twenty-nine or thirty states will be given to these states to help them start afresh to rebuild.

In any event this proposal is accepted, Nigerians will now look forward to the day when their states or local governments will be bigger as well as be sustainable. It will be able to generate an enough revenue on its own and not rely solely on the federal government for over 80 percent of its funds requirements. For example, each of these six or seven new states and local governments will show and prove that they can generate at least 80 percent of their revenue to be qualified as a state or a local government.

A law should be passed that will mandate that Nigerians will be accepted as citizens of any state or local government they call home, and also the word *nonindigene* should be banned from being used by any Nigerian to describe his or her fellow citizen in all parts of the nation as it is the case today.

After new states are created everybody will be treated equally no matter his or her tribe. In addition, Nigerians will be able to find and get states and local government jobs anywhere they live without discrimination as it is currently the case today.

Also, should the new six or seven states become successfully implemented, it will be good for the economics of Nigeria. Of course, many people will call this proposal crazy and unworkable in a nation where institutionalized tribalism, nepotism, favoritism, bribery, and corruption are the order of the day. It is still a hypothetical statement, but I urge all Nigerians to embrace this proposal if they are looking for a better unified country for everyone. Can you imagine the benefit and the outcome of joining different tribes and dialects together to form state and local government as one people and one nation? These states and local governments will no doubt, unlike before, benefit from a pool of talented, skilled, and creative individuals who will become citizens in all of the states.

The nation stand the chance of saving trillions of naira if six or seven state are created the money that can be used for rebuilding the country. This venture will help to fix the nation. Besides, the people will have a brand-new country!

Where Is the Nigerian Oil Money?

A few years ago, a former military commander and secretary of state, General Collin Powell, of the United States visited Nigeria. After a few days of visit, he raised an alarm on the poor living conditions he witnessed in the country, and he said this, "Nigerians have oil money but pissed it off." I agree with him 100 percent, and 99 percent of Nigerians agreed with him 100 percent as well, but few privileged Nigerian elites called him names and turned against him, attacked him for telling the truth about the economic state of the nation where billions and billions of dollars of the nation's wealth are stolen on a daily basis while leaving the masses to bite the nails. I and 99 percent of Nigerians thank him for caring and telling the truth. Sir, your observation of the nation's leadership's mismanaging and misusing of the people's wealth is 100 percent correct. I know you did this because you love the country and want it to do well. These few privileged elites accusing you for telling the truth are the ones responsible for the stealing and mismanaging of Nigerian oil wealth. They feared that you might have revealed their secrets to Nigerian people and the world, hence their attacks on you.

Nigeria Has the Biggest Government Ever

The federal government of Nigeria is too big and too large, which make it to be absolutely the king, the queen, unholy, ungodly, and unwelcome Father Christmas of the nation's purse. It is a waste pipe. It is the center of fraud and all types of fraud, bribery, and corruption. They created all kinds of frivolous ministries that only serve the purposes of those holding power and their families, friends, and cronies but none for the citizens of Nigeria.

Each succeeding government in Nigeria has formed the habit of creating ministry after ministry and agency after agency that favor those who are close to the corridors of power and as a way to siphon the oil wealth. The situation is so bad that yearly budget allocations to these ministries are mainly used to cover overhead costs. Anything left goes into the private pockets of officials. It is heartbreaking to hear that majority of poor applicants from poor families have to pay big amounts of bribes to officials for them to get a job. Many of these poor job applicants have been in the job market for more than twenty years after graduating from universities.

Downsizing and Fixing the Big Nigerian Federal Government

No one would ever disagree that the federal government of Nigeria needs to be downsized to a manageable level by cutting massive wasteful government spending to save the people's money and to build a better nation.

The hour has come for those in power to stop pissing off the nation's oil wealth and other natural resources. The hour has come to hold someone accountable to explain the whereabouts of the nation's oil wealth. The hour has come to rescue this nation from the vampires that are responsible for its economic failures. The hour has come for political socializations to end the old political order and the status quo. The hour has come to put Nigerians back to work. The hour has come for the nation's university graduates to find a job at least two years after graduation and not to wait for twenty years or forever. The hour has come to put back to work the nation's high school graduates who for more than thirty-seven years have never known what a job is. The hour has come for Nigerians to take back their country from its destroyers.

The hour has come for the masses to send a clear message to every leader among the old political order and their political appointees that their time is up and that they should start to pack their bags and baggages to leave, and they will never be allowed again to participate in politics in Nigeria. The hour has come for the masses to begin to benefit from their oil wealth. The hour has come for the end of tribalism, nepotism, favoritism, bribery, and corruption. The hour has come to write a better constitution for the people. The hour has come to create living wage jobs for Nigerians. The hour has come when this nation will be accounted among the technological world. The hour has come to build the critical infrastructures to move the nation's economy forward. The hour has come when the government will have to agree that a tree cannot make a forest and the nation needs to seek out trusted friends and allies around the globe to help them rebuild the nation's shattered economy. The hour has come that every child in this nation will receive a free universal primary and secondary education. The hour has come when no child will ever go to school barefoot or buy and carry their benches to school and back home. The hour has come when no child in this nation will ever go to bed or go to school with an empty stomach. The hour has come when every child attending public and private schools will be entitled to free breakfast and lunch every day at schools funded by governments. The hour has come when the nation's poor university students will get the federal government guaranteed student loans and free government grants and scholarships to help them pay for their education. The hour has come when every poor Nigerian will get a welfare check and free medical care in every part of the nation The hour has come when the nation's educational system will be torn down from the top to bottom and reformed and rebuilt. All the above listed actions are a part of the needed reforms in this nation.

Invalid Ministries and Agencies Marked for Elimination

The federal government created a bunch of irrelevant after irrelevant ministries and agencies that only favor the 1 percent privileged citizens. Some of them are leftovers from colonial masters that today are no longer relevant to the nation's economic growth and progress; instead it sabotages the political, social, and economic changes the country's economy needs to grow in modern time.

I found more than thirty ministries and bunch of agencies that most of them are not needed. The government waste trillions of naira every year to keep these on needed ministries.

The Old and Antiquated Colonial Office Positions to Go

The offices that have outlived its mandate and that require immediate closure are as follows: (1) the offices of the secretary to the federal government, (2) the offices of the head of services, and (3) the offices of the director general.

In fact, the offices of the secretary to the federal government and the offices of the head of services are absolutely no longer needed because they no longer serve their intended purposes after the end of colonial rule. What it does now is to drain away scarce resources that the nation doesn't have. The offices are also responsible for almost all the bad public policies and decrees enacted in the country for the past half a century. It is a master in bureaucracy delays.

The office of the director general will be downsized to become executive director to head each section of the ministry. The overall head of each ministry will be the minister, his assistant ministers, and duty ministers. The nation cannot afford to spend billions of naira annually to continue keep afloat offices that are no longer needed, which is also a clog in the wheel of progress.

The following reasons are why these offices are needed or necessary:

1. The secretary to the federal government. What does the president of the nation do? The president and the joint houses of assembly are responsible to make laws and run the country. Why then should the power to run the nation be delegated to this office? These three offices were colonial carryover used under the parliamentary system of government that is no longer needed under the democratic system of government.
2. The offices of head of service
3. The office of the director general (formerly called the offices of the permanent secretary). Sectional executive directors should be appointed to head each of these ministries on a one-on-one basis to work with the minister, assistant minister, and the deputy ministers.

Ministries not needed or emerged are as follows:

1. The ministry of Environment should become the Department of Environment Protection Agency (EPA) under a director and not a minister.
2. Ministry of Tranportation will take over the federal ministry of Aviation and Federal Aviation Administration (FAA) The Civil Aviation Authority should be within the ministry of Transportation.
3. The Federal Capital Territory Administration will be transferred to the District of Abuja if it is created.
4. The ministries of Industry, Trade, and Investment should be transfer to the Ministry of Commerce whose duty is to promote business, trade, investments, and administering of patent and census bureaus among others. A trade representative should be appointed work under the presidency.
5. The ministry of Youths Development, the ministry for Niger Delta and ministry of women affairs should become the Human Resources Administration (HRA) and should be handled on states and local governments level and should be under a director and not a minister that will serve all Nigerians in every state, city, suburb, and county with local offices.
6. The ministry of Culture, Tourism and Orientation will be the responsibility of states, local governments and the private sector.
7. Ministry of Works will become the ministry for Housing and Urban Development (HUD) to build affordable houses for all Nigerians.
8. Ministry of Mines and Power, ministry of Steels, Ministry of Petroleum and the Nigerian National Petroleum Corporation (NNPC) should be emerged with the

ministry of Energy(The Nigerian National Petroleum Corporation (NNPC) must be dissolved. The OPEC representative should have his office at the ministry of Energy offices.

9. Ministry of Water Resources should join the Environmental protection Agency [EPA] headed by a director not a minister. It should be handed over to the Environmental Protection Agency (EPA) after it is completely reformed. The water resources project will be under the new EPA department and under the care of a director and will work with local authorities to protect the environment and provide clean water for all.
10. The minister for Special Duties should be eliminated.
11. The ministry of Information, the ministry of Communication and ministry of Communication Technology should be replace with Federal Directorate of communications under a Director and not a minister. The president and other officials should hire spokesmen.
12. Ministry of Land, Housing, and Urban Development is another conduit for fraud and bribery and corruption. It should be replaced with the Ministry of Interior and Ministry for Housing and Urban Development in order to eliminate fraud, and they will be better handled at states, cities, suburbs, and counties levels while the federal while the federal government, states in conjunction with the local government will fund its development.

The ministry of Police Affairs should be eliminated. Federal police forces should become states and local government forces. After the new states and local governments will have their own, Police department, Fire department, EPA, Electricity, Supply, Water, and Social Service Department and so on and so forth. All hiring's must and should reflect the national character. This is to be discussed further.

The federal government of Nigeria should excuse itself from direct involvement in the oil field drilling, prospecting, and investing in refineries or managing of it. The federal government should enter into oil deal agreements with three reputable international oil companies to take charge of oil field drills and oil refineries and management because that is the best way the government can earn more oil money without any involvement in the physical aspect of the oil works or running rogue ministries and corporations. These oil companies have the technology, the finances, and the skills to run it better and more efficiently, which will help to save Nigerian people their money and wade off bribery and corruption and end bunkering. The federal government must enter into trade agreement with the countries of the international oil companies that may take over the management of the oil wells and refineries. It is also about time the federal government of Nigeria began to think about how to wane itself out of dependence on oil revenue for 98 percent of its budget. It is time to lay down plans for another alternative means of supplementing its oil revenue resources before it is too late.

13. The Ministry of Science and Technology has been created for more than forty years and has nothing to show that it ever existed. Nothing has been proven. Wasting money and time. It should be removed from ministry level office, to the office of science and technology policy under the presidency and run by an executive-director and not a minister.

14. Nigeria Institute of Research—I found out that there are sixty-six federal research institutes in Nigeria, and all are

funded by the federal government, and none is meeting its expectations. There is no scientific breakthrough to justify the money given to them except taking the country back to the seventeenth century. It is crazy that the federal government will waste such a huge amount of the nation's hard-earned money to fund sixty-six research centers.

Let me reveal what the two research centers I picked to examine are doing:

a. PRODA (Projects Development Institute, Enugu)—This institute has been operating for more than forty years. I checked their website and saw the items they claim to have discovered and produced are some expired, long-used local instruments that were first used in 1700. You wonder why the government spends such a huge amount of oil money to have the supposed Nigerian scientists make such instruments like mugs, bricks, garri-maker, are produced with crude technology-which some uneducated local roadside artisan in Nigeria could produce with less amount of money and time. That the federal government is spending billions of naira for such common things to be produced by the research centers is crazy. What they produce are not exportable and even not in high demand in the Nigerian local market. And they can't bring in any revenue to the government, cannot change a single life in the nation, and cannot help the economy to grow. It is just a complete waste of the people's hard-earned money. When I first heard of PRODA, I rejoiced with the hope that it was going to be the Nigerian Silicon Valley, but now I am dead wrong about my prediction.

FIRO (Federal Institute of Research, Oshodi)—This is among the two out of the sixty-six research centers that I chose to comment on. The institute boasted of a major discovery of cassava flour as the best flour to make bread. And it became another ridiculous claim of scientific breakthrough in the twenty-first century. The research institute was established more than forty years ago and yet hasn't become the nation's dreamed "Silcom Valley". Unfortunately no smart phones among other modern technology has been produced.

b. The Federal Institute of Research Oshodi [FIRO] recently announced the discovering of cassava flour after more than forty years of research. Because of this the nation's finance minister was so happy that she announced to the world about the cassava flour breakthrough. She enthusiastically entice the nation's bread bakers with seventy percent loan forgiveness if they convert their flour baking machine to cassava flour baking machine. This loan forgiveness merit a probe. Wonders, they say, will never seize occurring in Nigeria in different colors, shapes, and sizes. Why the sudden interest for a cassava that has been around for more than six hundred million years and was brought to Nigerian by missionaries from Mexico, North America. It is a food that lacks proteins and is usually consumed by the poorest of the poor, who are also looking for a way out of eating cassava if they could afford a better proteinous food, and now the government is forcing them to consume cassava bread without detailing its nutrition facts and values. Cassava or no cassava, anyone could guess that cassava is the lowest of the list of issues among catalogues of problems staring the country in its face. There are great many ways to invest this billions of naira that the government is giving to those men and women who will never honestly use the loans for its intended purposes but instead will steal it and bank it into their private account and will never repay a penny of it.

What are the reasons why the federal government created sixty-six research institutes? Tribalism is the major reason why the federal government of Nigeria created sixty-six institutes of research almost in every state. The reason is nothing but tribalism. Excellence, intelligence, talents, skills, creativity, and technology that are required for the better use of these institutes were sacrificed at the altar of tribalism. Every tribe and state were given two or more institutes whether it was needed or not. First and foremost, research centers are better run and managed by private sector's interest with better result. I urge the federal government to abolish all the research institutes now and commit all the resources and funds that are wasted here to something better that will provide better quality of life with direct impact on the masses' well-being. The government should have their hands off and let the private sector take over research centers with the help of international scientists. Though these are not the type of research centers Nigerian scientists need to succeed because they lack the critical modern sophisticated infrastructures that are not yet within the reach of the nation. No one can blame these Nigerian scientists because it is the fault of the federal government, who entrenched itself in every issue in the name of tribalism, which, at the end of the day, makes nothing work. The Nigerian scientists are doing their best with what they have. The blame goes to the federal government that likes to control everything that moves in Nigeria and has the habit of not getting anything done well. Can anyone tell Nigerians why the federal government of Nigeria shunned the infusion of the private sector will help to expand the economic growth development in the nation's economy? One may think that Nigeria is a socialist state.

15. Ministry of Mines and Steel Development (eliminated) was a project that was started in the seventies with the best intentions for Nigeria. However, down the line at one time, it became one of the biggest nightmares for Nigerian people. It will go down in the history of Nigeria as one of the biggest industrial frauds and corruptions to happen in this nation. Billions and billions of dollars of oil money vanished from here. At one time the projects were abandoned completely. As the nation begins its reforms, this project will be sold to willing international steel developers in the private sector economy. Should be emerged with Ministry of Energy and only the Ministry of Energy will exist.
16. Ministry for Communication Technology—What for? This should be eliminated.
17. Ministry of Sports will be left in the hands of sports businessmen and women and schools. The federal and states governments should no longer bank roll sports developments. The local governments should work with private sports developers to develop sports in the country. Sports developments should be eliminated from federal involvements. The government should hand this over to private sports investors. It is a big revenue earner if handled on the private sector levels. Government has been throwing money under the pit in the name of sports developments and should be ended.
18. Ministry of Nigerian Delta Affairs—Does this new addition to an already overloaded government make sense at all? These people are clamoring for their share of the oil money discovered in their backyards, but nothing was given to them. Instead of settling with them and giving them money through the banks, the government created

another large wasteful ministry that will cost billions and billions of naira, which will eventually end up in private bank accounts while the people will continue to cry for help without anyone listening.

19. The Sanitation Day should be eliminated. It causes the nation's economy billions of naira. Everyone knows that sanitation departments are responsible for keeping the country clean and neat. It is the responsibility of the local governments and not the masses. The idea to shut down the nation twice a week because of sanitation is economically counterproductive and must be discontinued.

The following agencies and programs are outdated or are not meeting their expectations. They will either be eliminated, changed, or modified:

1. JAMB (The Joint Admission Matriculation Board)—It is an empire of fraud and corruption that should be eliminated or changed because its intended purpose has been defeated through bribery and corruption.
2. The sub-continental and national high school diploma required to graduate from high school, such as the West Africa Certificate of Education [WACE], The London Certificate of Education [GCE] and the National Certificate of Education [NICO] is antiquated and should be discontinued.Sudents should earn their high diploma from the schools they attended. A waste of time for the children, a system tainted with fraud, bribery, and corruption, The government should look into the fraud tainted high school diploma awards in the country. However, the solution to this problems is to discontinue the current test-

ing system because it is counterproductive that produces certificate forgers.

3. The Nigerian law school was established by the colonial masters at the time when there was no school in the country offering law courses. In order to help Nigerians who took the London law correspondence courses to gain practical knowledge after graduation was basically the reason the law school was established. The federal government should not continue to waste money to keep these law schools operating because almost every university in the country offers law degree courses today. Money is needed to build critical infrastructures that will bring jobs for these graduates.

I have successfully identified most of the federal government's economic policies that make it impossible for the government to govern or control the policies that turn out to be a huge waste of the nation's wealth. These policies largely favor the privileged few elites in Nigeria and disfavor the majority, practically being responsible in creating massive sufferings for the masses. I have either eliminated, changed, or modified some of the ministries and agencies so as to make it possible for Nigerians to benefit from all federal and state programs. The other benefits of these reforms is that it will make government smaller and more responsible, efficient, smarter, and more beneficial to the people. It will help cut down on fraud, bribery, and corruption.

The ministries selected to continue to function as an entity or join together with another ministry or ministries are as follows:

1. Ministry of Defense
2. Ministry of Agriculture

3. Ministry of Education
4. Ministry of Finance
5. Ministry of External Affairs
6. Ministry of Interior
7. Ministry of Health
8. Ministry of Justice
9. Ministry for Transportation
10. Ministry of Energy
11. Ministry of Commerce (to promote business and trade, administer patent and census bureaus, promote sales of Nigerian products abroad, etc.)
12. Labor Ministry (to oversee federal workplace and employment programs and regulations, is a new addition)
13. Ministry of Interior

I have picked up thirteen ministries from the original list of thirty federal cabinet level posts to remain as they were created. But about eighteen of these ministries will either be merged or completely be eliminated. Reforms will in no doubt save the federal, states and local governments trillions of naira.

These previous ministries will be merged as follows:

1. Petroleum Ministry, Ministry of Mines and Power, Ministry of Steel Development, Nigerian National Petroleum Corporation, and the OPEC representative will be under the Ministry of Energy. It is only the energy ministry that will be active, but none will be permitted to engage in oil field prospecting or drilling or even see or handle the oil revenue.
Ministry of Science and Technology should be eliminated and transferred to the Presidency Office of Science and Technology Policy Department.

2. Ministry of Water Resources will be under the Environmental Protection Agency.
3. Ministry for Police Affairs should be eliminated and end the federal police force as an end to an era. The office of the federal inspector general of police and all related forces should be ended and its reins handed over to the states and local governments who form the new security forces for the sake of efficiency and cost cutting. The nation no longer requires colonial-style security forces. The Nigerian law enforcement agencies should be fragmented for accountability. The Nigerian law enforcement agencies should be operating under states governors, the city, suburbs, county, and suburban. The governors and the majors will be responsible for hiring and firing police rank and file. More discussion on this issue will continue inside the paper.
4. Ministry for Communications, Ministry of Information, Radio Nigerian, Nigerian Television Authority, and Ministry for Communication Technology go to prove that there are too many information ministries. All of them should face the chopping block in order to save Nigerian oil money and commit it to the areas where it will benefit the masses. The job of these information ministries has been covered using the post of the presidential spokesman, congressional spokesman, governor's spokesman. Therefore, these ministries should be the responsibility of the private sector, and the federal government should not invest money into these pits. At best, these information ministries should be merged to form the new Federal Communication Commission or Directory of Federal Communications and will be headed by a director and supporting staff.

5. Ministry of Works should be transferred to Ministry of Transportation. The new Ministry for Housing and Urban Development will replace Ministry of Works.
6. The Aviation Ministry will no longer be a full-time ministry. It will be placed under the Ministry of Transportation but will have an administrative office under a director
7. Ministry of Sports should be dissolved. Sports is supposed to be a moneymaking venture, but government has been spending billions of naira every year to support it without any returns, and it should be in the hands of private investors. Schools and private investors will be in charge of developing sports activities both internally and externally. Interested foreign sports developers may apply. Also, cities, suburbs, and counties will be responsible in partnering with private sports owners to build stadiums through selling shares and collecting taxes.
8. Ministry for Women Affairs and Social Development, Ministry for Niger Delta Affairs, Ministry for Youth Development are three high-sounding names. You don't need a soothsayer to tell you these ministries are set up to defraud innocent citizens. How can a serious, reasonable government do something like this to its people by claiming that it cares for their welfare but only uses ministries to steal from the people? These ministries must be investigated. These three ministries should be uprooted, destroyed, and replaced with HRA. The Human Resources Administration is directed towards helping the poor and the youths and should be under states, cities, counties, and suburbs.
9. The Federal Capital Territory should be dissolved because it has overstayed its mandates, and it has been known to engage in massive land and housing fraud. It will be

audited and probed. It will be transferred to create Stone Mountain or Rocky Mountain District of Abuja State

10. Ministry of Culture and Tourism and Orientation will no longer be under federal government and will go to states, cities, suburbs, and counties including private tourism owners
11. Ministry for Specialist Duties should be dissolved. It is a waste of money.
12. Ministry of Land, Housing, and Urban Development will have its head chopped off. It will become the new Ministry of Housing and Urban Development.

The Nigerian Police Forces Reforms and the End of the Post of the Inspector General of Nigerian Police Forces

Every Nigerian is aware that tribalism may be one of the major contributing factors to the forming of the national police forces, which has turned out to be a national disaster, embarrassment, and shame for the country. I am sure that the colonial masters never left behind a national police force. It was created by Nigerian leaders because of tribalism. The police today benefit from expired technology from Europe. Ethics is a serious issue in the law enforcement agency. The federal system of law enforcement agencies must be dismantled to be replaced with state, city, county, suburb, and municipality system of police departments. The process of building modern law enforcement agencies under the legal system in the nation will begin.

I think Robert Peel, the founder of the London Metropolitan Police Force in 1829, if he was alive today, would be ashamed of the Nigerian police force today. The Nigerian police functioned very well with some degree of honesty and integrity after its British administrators handed them over to their Nigerian administrators, until it became politicized by military rules beginning from 1976.

The forces became deeply involved in politics leading to some of them being appointed state governors and federal ministers. Instead of doing the jobs they were hired to do, which is protecting the safety of the general public, they choose politics instead of protecting the people and the nation and are still at it up till today. After the departure of the colonial masters, bribery and corruption began to firmly grip the Nigerian police forces and its auxiliaries to the point of helplessness. Wearing official government uniforms is not a permission to ask and receive bribes or insult and beat up your fellow citizens. The Nigerian police forces was modeled according to the London Metropolitan Police Forces, which is nicked name "Met or Old Bill" which remains one of the finest polices in the world, unlike their counterparts in Nigeria.

The Inspector General of Police

The era of the national inspector general of the Nigerian police forces should come to an end. All uniformed civilian police forces will no longer be under the control of the federal government or be called national police forces. The forces to be affected are the Nigerian police force and the mobile police force; these two are armed and have the power to arrest, detain, and prosecute Other forces that will be no longer be national or under the control of federal government are the road safety, the traffic wardens, and the civil defense. These forces and other auxiliary forces will be the responsibility of the states, cities, suburbs, and counties. The state police department will be under the governor. The city, suburb, and county police departments will be under the major. The new federal marshal will be stationed within the federal seat of power because of the newly created district of Abuja. The district of Abuja will have its own police department, which may be named ADPD (Abuja District Police Department, Abuja).

By downsizing the current states and creating new six to seven states, cities, counties, and suburbs will become responsible to hire, train, and fire police officers. A commissioner of police will head the police departments, and they will be under the city, suburb, and county majors. This new arrangement will help to eliminate the previous ineffective one-million-man Nigerian police forces and save money. It will be smaller and more efficiently managed. Police officers will once again be proud of their jobs and themselves. They will be well trained, well-mannered, and well compensated. Police officers should be grounded on ethics and moral and cultural awareness. They will once again be able to earn respect from the general public. The New York City Police Department could be of help in training new police officers. NYPD (New York City Police Department) and LAPD (Los Angeles City Police Department), for example, are specialists in forming state, city, suburb, and county police forces. They will help in planning and training the new modern Nigerian police forces.

Education Reforms

There is nowhere in the world that you can find anybody who deliberately underestimates the importance of a good and a well-rounded and sound education and its contributions to a nation and world developments. At least, America and the Western world can attest to it. Fredrick Douglass, a former slave who taught himself how to read and write, can attest it, and China, Japan, and India will agree, and Nigeria and African nations know it yet choose to maintain eighteenth-century educational systems. Today, we live in a globalized world; any country anywhere in the world is just one second away from the next country. Because of this possibility, the world is grateful to giants like Microsoft, IBM, Apple, Google, Facebook, Yahoo, YouTube, AT&T, and Verizon, just to name a few. It is time for Nigeria to join the global world and the global economy that will help them to transform their educational system and their economic systems into the twenty-first-century world economy. The goal and vision is about the future, the world will see Nigerian children become educated inventors and innovators that will let them become part of the family of world changers. Nigerians, it is time to reverse course and change the way and the method knowledge is currently being imparted to children in the nation. It is time to provide quality and qualitative free education to all Nigerian children.

The Nigerian system of education must be critically analyzed and reformed.

Ibadan University was founded in 1948 by the colonial masters and became the first Nigerian premier university. Educated Nigerian luminaries like China Achebe, the author of *Things Fall Apart*, and Wole Soyinka, the author of *The Man Died* and a winner of the Nobel Literature Prize, are alumni. Later along the line, the University of Nsukka and the University of Ife followed and were founded by Nigerians and were considered to be the nation's Ivy League universities back then. The colonial masters, the missionaries, and the private school developers had the noblest of ideas for a well-rounded education, leading their efforts to build prestigious high schools and secondary schools around the country that were well equipped with the best teachers, staffs, and tutoring materials you could find anywhere in world then. Today in Nigeria, such prestigious institutions from pre-K to twelfth grades and institutions of higher learning no longer can be found because they were wickedly declared dinosaurs in 1977 by a leader who senselessly introduced an educational decree that was responsible for bringing down the nation's educational system, as it was known those days.

The year was 1976 when Obasanjo replaced his boss, who was killed in yet another botched military coup in Nigeria. After assuming the responsibility as the head of state, there was the daunting task of unifying a broken nation, but whether that was achieved, no one can tell.

Once the head of state was killed during the latest aborted coup, Nigerians had lost hope about the future of the nation because they had loved and trusted the murdered head of state to move the country to the right direction. However, having no choice, they were bound to support the new military leader whether they agreed with him or not. He was a soldier with a gun. Throughout when the new leader began his transitioning to his new role as a head of state, the fate of the nation was hanging in the balance, not knowing the man and what to expect from his leadership

There was high and lower hope about him. Some Nigerians mounted oppositions against him. People like Fela, the Nigerian music icon, was strongly opposed to his leadership. The head of state's reaction to Fela's opposition resulted to the death of Fela's mother and the burning down of her house. Many conflicts followed the head of state due to his too many unpopular decrees he introduced to the nation. Many Nigerians did not see anything special in his decrees that were ever capable of moving the nation to the right direction, but rather, what they saw were decrees that came to set the nation further backward from where the nation was before he claimed power.

One out of his so many unproductive decrees that hit the center nerves of the Nigerian people's mental psyche was his decree on education decreed in 1977. That was the last straw that broke the camel's back. The Nigerian educational system faced an unknown future after he decreed that books of any type will no longer be imported.

There was no immediate plan to fill those gaps by Nigerian authors. Nigerians witnessed bookstore after bookstore shutting their doors. Notable among them was CMS Bookstore in Lagos, the most popular and the biggest bookstore in the nation that can be compared with Barnes & Noble of the United States. I watched and cried as it shut its doors. Libraries closed their doors due to lack of books and materials. It was an educational anarchy against the nation by a one-man bandit. That moronic 1977 education decree has not been completely corrected, and the educational system has been infiltrated with fraud of all kinds and bribery and corruption. The head of state was a soldier you dared not challenge, or you will be close to your early grave. After all, he slaughtered many of his fellow high-ranking military officers for the insane excuse that they planned to overthrow his government.

His educational decree allowed the federal government to take over all the schools in the country. The resulting was the sacking of missionaries and private school developers and teachers, which turned out to be counterproductive for the nation's educational system. His decree made the nation's once progressive educational system as it was known then to fall flat on its face. Once high-flying universities like Ibandan, Nsukka, and Ife became shadows of its previous self because most of its foreign professors and teaching equipment became short, and experienced university and high school administrators were forced to leave the country on the orders of the Nigerian authority. Whether the decree was a good idea or not, no one can tell, but everyone knows that it was very premature and very early to take such measures against a nation that was just coming out of a war and was trying to rebuild, and education is one of the basic foundations that should have been solidly laid for the future of the nation. Some of the nation's once prestigious high schools are today in tatters. To make matters worse, he invited Nigerian scholars who studied and were living abroad back home to take over universities, some as administrators and others as teachers. Many of them were brought from Eastern Bloc and other overseas countries. For example, some returned from Russia and the West, and many of them laid claim to having several PhDs and many other degrees. If you take a closer look at the decrees the head of state had enacted, it looks very similar to what you can expect from communist nations. An example was his nationalization policy. Though he never declared Nigeria a communist nation, his actions and deeds spoke volumes. Under his similar communist autocratic decrees the really communist nations fared 100 percent better economically than Nigeria during his time in office.

No sooner than these scholars returned home from abroad, Nigerians had the highest hope that they will help make the nation's educational system right again by restoring sanity and intellectualism in the nation's educational school systems. However, surprisingly, they were more concerned about their personal ambitions (status) than rebuilding the nation's broken-down educational system, which was the primary reason they were called back home. They became married to the media to help them promote their false egos; they fought each other over university positions and titles like chair professor. To be called a professor in Nigerian universities is a big deal because it is considered a life achievement. To vie for the chair professor, you must have a PhD and be prepared to fight in order to earn this title. It is also considered a permanent life title that you can attach to your name.

A *professor* is defined as a teacher or an instructor, may be referred to as a professor of history, professor of English, and so on and so forth. No one can believe that in the quest to attain the professorship chair, many of them died mysteriously. Every teacher is a professor. It is a shame and sad that these elites are very mean-spirited. The university professors seem very pompous, mean, and arrogant that they can a punish students who mistakenly fail to address them as a professor or Dr. So-and-So if he or she has a PhD. They neglected to do the job they were hired to do; instead, they succeeded beyond reasonable doubt to run down higher institutions of studies in the country. You wonder why a learned person who is expected to be cultured and mannered will descend as low as to pad himself or herself with such worldly titles like His or Her Excellency, Honorable, doctor, professor, chief, engineer, barrister, reverend, and so on and so forth. They wish to be known and be addressed in this manner as a symbol of success, status, and as well to appear as VIPs in order for them to earn respect in the society. Actions speak louder than voice. These are groups of privileged elites who are responsible for mismanaging the nation's schools and everything they laid their hands upon. They misappropriated any position of trust and authority given to them to hold and help develop the country. They masterly abused their powers to the detriment of Nigerian majority who face hardships every day.

These guys were not done after fighting for professor chairs and running down all the existing universities handed over to them, they dubiously injected tribalism into the university system. Every one of them wanted to be relevant. Every one of them wanted to be a head of university, polytechnics, or college of education or university of science and technology in their states of origin and wanted to become a university vice chancellor, provost, or professor, just to name a few, whether he or she is competent or not. For them to achieve their diabolical plans, they invaded the head of state, the military governors, and ministers and convinced them about their state's lack of inadequate classrooms. They also were able to convince the federal government and state government to build two to three institutions of higher learning and federal government secondary schools. These ideas may appear to be robust thinking, but for heaven's sake, did they ever think about the critical infrastructures needed for this venture to work for the people? For sure, such ideas were never considered or placed on the table.

It is now absolutely clear that the Nigerian leadership and their enablers care only for themselves but not for the importance of providing quality and quantitative education that will be conducted on a healthy, conducive, and clean learning environment for students. What these men and women did with the future of education in this country is not fit to print. The damage their foolish wisdoms did to education in this country is still hurting the future of education in the country. As earlier mentioned, regardless of whether critical infrastructures existed or not, their latest move was to blanket every state with the codes designed in tribal names as a means of assigning new universities of science and technology and polytechnic, which often took root from run-down houses to educate Nigerian future leaders. Though they may claim that the using of run-down houses for schools was to ease admission problems, the problems have multiplied since then. To secure admission into higher institutions of learning after high school graduation is difficult it could be compared to someone who is constantly trying to collect water with a basket, and the biggest nightmare that faces many Nigerian high school graduates and their parents is sometimes it takes some of them five years after to get admitted, when their parents or guardians might have paid hefty bribes to officials. There are serious, serious university classroom shortages because the federal government and state government hijacked education, and they seem incapable of making a single one of them right, hence the low quality of education. The issue of poor education has not been widely discussed because the government pays little attention to it, and the university teachers' union pays little attention as well but rather chooses to demand salary increase after salary increase year in and year out, which often lead to the shutting down of schools for months, if not years. That is not the way to acquire a good education. The government should stop toying with the future of the children's educational success. The leadership has constantly offered Band-Aid solutions to the shortages of classrooms and qualified teachers. Over one million qualified high school students are unable to gain admission to universities every year. Leadership in the country continues to pay lip service and has a nonchalant attitude towards the education of the nation's future leaders. The educational system is the type that wants to hire Davis Guggenheim (*Waiting for Superman*). Please give a call to Geoffrey Canada, the founder of the Harlem Schoolchildren Zone to help rescue Nigerian education.

Fixing Nigerian Education

Education should be considered top priority and should be tackled head-on. The first thing to do is to stop the federal government from interfering in the day-to-day physical management of schools in the nation if efficiency is to be attained and achieved.

The federal government's major responsibilities are to fund, regulate, and set the standard benchmark for education developments for the state, city, suburb, and county. Funding public schools from PK4 to institutions of higher learning should be a joint effort among the federal government, state government, and local governments. Also, the federal government standard benchmark will affect private schools' developments as well.

The federal government will no longer be in charge to appoint school administrators whether at universities or at secondary schools. All the existing federal universities and secondary schools should be handed over to the states, cities, suburbs, and counties to be managed by them.

Each state can own and run one university in their state's capital while the majority of the schools will be built and run by local governments and private sectors. The federal government and the state government will send educational fund allocations to local governments that extend free universal education throughout the country. JAMB should no longer be under the federal government's control but rather will be assigned to an independent body such as the private sector. WAEC, GCE, and NICO should be discontinued. With the federal government out of school management, it will bring about the end of tribalism, nepotism, favoritism, and discrimination in the nation's school system. Making testing of students after five years a national certificate issue has resulted to certificates fraud, bribery, and corruption, making some female students engage in illegal sex with officials in order to obtain certificates. Students enrolled in the nation's public and private school system will be given free breakfast and lunch while at school and must be made compulsory. The nation's children deserve to be cared for because the oil wealth belongs to them too. I repeat, every child in the nation will receive free universal primary and secondary education. The government has absolutely no excuse to give to these parents and their children. The government can afford to give free education and free breakfast and lunch in schools in an oil-rich nation is nothing but a complete fallacy.

All national, subcontinental, and international examinations, which include the West African Examination Council (WAEC), the General Certificate of Education (GCE), a London certificate and the latest addition called the National Certificate (NC), imposed on students an order to earn a high school diploma, which is outdated and should be wiped out and discontinued. These series of examinations imposed on the children of West African nations during the colonial rule should be padlocked and the keys thrown away forever.

It is unthinkable to mention that these children will spend five painful years studying only to end up sitting for intercontinental and national certificates examinations that are almost worthless after obtaining them because they cannot find a job with it or gain admission into institutions of higher learning.

Determination alone is omnipotent; therefore, a single one-time test given to students after five years of high school education or after four years of university education is not the best way to assess students' intellectual abilities. It has been found that about 80 percent of students failed these tests.

And when they fail, they resort to buying certificates. This is one of the primary reasons why certificates are bought and sold in the country. At the completion of the education reforms, all schools tests will be conducted internally in every school and in each student's classroom.

The metric to be used to test and measure students' progress is called cumulative (GPA) tests, which will start from the day a child enters school till the day he graduates. He will begin to earn his grades after each test. At the end of every term the quarter students will receive their grades in the school until he or she graduate with a certificate or not. They should be no external test for student to graduate with high school diploma. If a student makes A, his test score will be 90–100 percent and marked Excellent; 84–89 percent is B+, 80–83 percent is B, 75–80 percent is C and C+ and marked Fair. The school will determine what will be the lowest and highest GPA that a student needs to earn in order to graduate a class and to earn his or her high school diploma or university diploma at the end of their final year in school. The minimum passing grade should be set at 2.5 point grade average [GPA]. A 4.0 grade point. Any student who earns the highest grade is said to have graduated on top of his or her class. With this in mind, there is absolutely no need for Nigerian universities to indiscriminately award students too many first class, second class, and third class degrees. No one knows for sure how many students are awarded these first, second, and third class degrees in a class. This system of grading students is an antiquated system that must be abolished. Must be discontinued. In addition, students will no longer take part in any type of external examinations outside the classroom.

Test taking appears be too excessive and too dictatorial and oppressive and antiquated, which has not served the receiver the intended purposes or neither gave the nation the best educated men and women needed to run the country well. Note that the education that is being offered is not so great, yet it is so frustrating for parents and students to have an easy access to get it. The math and English credit requirements before a student can gain admission into institutions of higher learning should be abolished. All school tests, works, and grading will begin right away in his or her classroom the very day a child begins schooling until they are graduated or drop out. There should be no more external tests outside the school classrooms. Kids need jobs after finishing their education, not having their certificates buried after graduation.

What is the purpose of education?

> The function of education is to teach one to think intensively and to think critically. But education which stops with efficiency may prove the greatest menace to society. The most dangerous criminal may be the man gifted with reason but no morals. We must remember that intelligence is not enough. Intelligence plus character—that is the goal of education. (Martin Luther King Jr., a speech at Morehouse College, Atlanta, 1948)

The purpose of education has changed from that of producing a literate society to that of producing a learning society. (Margaret Ammos, associate secretary of ASCD, October 1964)

The main purpose of the American school is to provide for the fullest possible development of each learner for living morally, creatively, and productively in a democratic society. (The ASCD committee on platform of beliefs educational leadership, January 1957)

To prepare children for citizenship
Thttp://www.merriam-webster.com/o cultivate a skilled workforce
To teach cultural literacy
To help students become critical thinkers
To help students compete in a global marketplace (http://www.forbes.com/sites/sap/2012/08/15/what is the purpose of education)

It's Ever Changing

In his book *A Whole New Mind*, Daniel Pink argues that, as a society, we have transcended the so-called Knowledge Age and are now in a Conceptual Age, where our problems no longer have a single verifiable answer. Success in the Knowledge Age was mainly determined by a "SAT-ocracy," a series of tests throughout the education system that required logic and analysis to identify a single correct answer. This does not meet the need of the Conceptual Age, which requires creativity, innovations, and design skills. He further asserts that education is still firmly geared towards the needs of the Information Age, quickly disapproving era. It's as if our children are moving along an assembly line, where we diligently instill math, reading, and science skills and then test them to see how much they retained, making sure they meet all the "standards" of production. Today, a successful member of society must bring something different to the table. Individuals are valued for their unique contributions and their ability to think creatively, take initiative, and incorporate a global perspective into their decisions

Looking at the above opinions, it seems to me that Nigerian educational system has no purpose and no goals other than to tell the kids who graduated high school that he or she did not credit mathematics and English and so cannot gain admission in a university even though they have passed the two subjects. Why would education be based only on tests after tests that have not benefitted these children or the nation?

Making crediting of Mathematics and English as a mandatory requirements to gain admission into universities is counterproductive to education. It appears that ignorance runs deep among educationists in Nigeria because they failed to articulate the best way to educate and test children. What type of education does the authority plan to give to these children? Why did the authority design an education system that does not allow a high school graduate to be admitted in a university because he did not credit English and mathematics even though they passed these subjects? Can every student earn A or B in a test?

These kids are then sent back to school to retake the same eight subjects they had already passed. The outcome of retaking these examinations is that parents and kids will resort to examination fraud to meet these requirements. The idea to punish innocent children who already have graduated high school with a lame excuse that they did not have A and B in mathematics and English is wrong as well as counterproductive and should be stopped now. This process made the kids buy certificates. The authority must end erroneous beliefs that every child must have A or B in mathematics and English before they qualify to be admitted in an institution of higher learning. The authority should stop turning the nation's potential leaders into certificates criminals through their backwards thinking.

The ban on importation of books and materials affected the educational system in no small ways.Businesses were also affected and have made it hard for high school graduates to find jobs after graduation. University graduates face an uncertain future in the job market. Painfully enough for more than thirty something years now, high school graduates can no longer find a job. The entry-level jobs which usually were reserved for high school graduates are now the best jobs university graduates can find if they are lucky and it is available.

What is the purpose of university and secondary school education in Nigeria? Many university students who graduated since 1995 have never found one decent job. High school graduates since 1985 never find a job with their high school diploma. So why did they go to school? How do you build a progressive nation with this type of situation? Like Martin Luther King Jr. said, "But education which stops with efficiency may prove the greatest menace to society." The most dangerous criminal may be the man gifted with reason but no morals. Ask any Nigerian whether there is any moral left in Nigerian society today since after 1977, when wicked decrees were imposed by a leader upon his nation, which set the hands of the clock backwards for a growing, progressing economy before he came to power. Ever since then, ethics and morals are at the lowest ebb in the nation today and is affecting the educated and uneducated Nigerians. About 80 percent of Nigerians take to petty trading, and some take to crime in order to survive. Thousands if not millions are fleeing the country in order to escape poverty, therefore causing the nation to lose its potentials on a daily basis.

The greatest problem facing education in the country today is the issue of technology. University students, high school students, and primary school students study with lanterns and torches at night and do their homework in an oil-rich nation. Shame, shame, and shame on Nigerian leaders!

As bad as these conditions are, how do you tell someone about ethics and morals or talk about good behavior, honesty, and decency when their leaders themselves are not? The 1 percent ruling class and their family, cronies, and friends continue to loot and accumulate unjust riches with the people's oil wealth. It is time to say enough is enough. It is time to uproot, destroy, and rebuild bigger, better, and stronger. It is time. Nigerians deserve better.

Nigerian Professionals

All professional board of examinations will no longer be conducted by the federal government educational agencies, rather by the to-be created state's board of education. In the future all professional board of examinations should be conducted by states board of education in the following professions, medical, law, pharmacy, engineering, accounting, nursing and teachers all must be certified by the state board of education and not the federal government ministry of education. They must be state certified in order to practice.

Teachers Certification Examination

Every future teacher must be certified professionally before he or she will be permitted to teach. A law should be passed to make it against the law for anyone to teach without being certified as a teacher. And such individuals must have a BSc degree with teacher's education in order to qualify to take the teachers' state board examination. After two years of teaching, he or she is expected to have an MSc degree. The state board examination can be taken in any state of the candidate's choice and will be valid throughout the nation. It is a mandatory examination for anyone who wants to teach.

These professional bodies will be involved in setting the standard benchmark for the tests. The Nursing Council Board will continue to exist but will be no longer bankrolled by the federal government. The federal government will no longer be directly physically involved in conducting any of these examinations. Rather, the professional bodies will team up with the state's board of education to set goals, standards, and benchmarks for testing. Modify the current existing standards to reflect modern education testing standards. Professional examinations can be held as many times as possible in a month. They will be no discrimination against anyone.

Professional Teachers' Education

No one knows exactly the last time when there was training for professional teachers in the country. I mean modern twenty-first-century teachers whose ages might not be more than forty-five years old. I am aware that teachers' training colleges are no longer in existence, which I believed was a good policy for closing them. I also know that there are colleges of education in every state, but I am not sure if they are producing enough secondary school teachers and if the equipment to do so is up-to-date. But I still wonder how someone can attend a college of education and after three years of studies, he or she is awarded the NCE (National Certificate of Education) just one year short of earning a BSc degree in education. I considered it a waste of money and time since these graduates cannot teach in universities. What I believe the government can do is nothing but to merger college of education with various universities in the country and designate them as teachers academy; at which time these future professional teachers will benefit from university level courses. From here a prospective student will have the opportunity to earn his or her BSc, MSc, or PhD with course specializations. Probably all future students will study with full scholarships in order to feed the school system with qualified and modern school teachers that will teach from PK4 to university. The government, which includes the federal, the state, city, county, and suburbs, will have to draw a plan to fund and train ten thousand to twenty thousand professional schoolteachers for at least the next ten years, and all will study with federal grants and scholarships. Doing this will benefit the nation and the children. There will be no more federal-government-owned schools of any type, but through the federal ministry of education, it will continue to fund education with contributions from state, city, suburbs who will be in charge of managing schools. There should be no more national or intercontinental certificate examinations for high school students of any type in Nigeria.

Getting professional, qualified teachers is one of the biggest issues facing education in Nigeria at all levels. The nation's leaders are aware about the serious shortage of teachers and pretend as if it doesn't exist, but no one has come up with solutions because the government is using the services of poorly paid, untrained graduate teachers, who after twenty years of graduating from university, cannot find jobs.

For the past twenty years or thereabout, due to endemic unemployment opportunities in the country, many graduates who perhaps have been on the job market for more than twenty years have turned to teaching due to lack of other job opportunities in order to keep mind and soul together. Though they are poorly paid and untrained, there is no other choice for them. Is the government not aware about the dangers of using largely untrained teachers that will definitely hurt academic standard? To fill the gaps of teacher shortages, government may consider hiring foreign-trained teachers, particularly in the areas of science and technology. Every teacher anywhere in the country must be board certified before they can be permitted to teach. Federal-government-guaranteed loans, scholarships, and grants should be given to those who want to become teachers to study.

Standard for Schools Development

School reforms should include a standard requirement redeveloping the current existing schools or constructing new schools. Private school developers will be mandated to show and prove that they are professionally qualified and have the financial means to build and maintain a high school, private primary school, kindergarten, and university. An initial deposit of at least two hundred million naira is required to start a new secondary and primary school. At least the sum of fifty million naira is required to redevelop existing schools. Individuals who want to develop a brand-new university should show and prove their professional ability to do so as well as show at least the sum of one billion naira. Important requirements are well-staffed schools, water, and twenty-four-hour electricity supply. Five hundred million naira is required to redevelop existing schools.

The JSS (Junior Secondary School) and SSCE (Senior Secondary Certificate Education)

A former federal minister of education attempted to reform education but instead made matters worse when he created twin secondary school system. His idea to have two high schools in one compound, one called junior and another called senior, and add one year extended the time of graduation, which served no particular purpose. This idea only helped to drain the scarce resources from the already cash-starved school system. What is the purpose of having two school principals in one high school? Does the idea of adding one more year of schooling favor the children, or does it save money? At the same time, the educational standards remain at the level of nineteenth century. The schoolchildren are already overburdened with an educational system that doesn't work for them. The goal of any reform should be to reverse the burdensome way the educational system is currently established. The system of educating functional illiterates should be changed.

If you factor in the added cost to run the newly created twin secondary schools system, which was absolutely unnecessary, I believe that money earmarked to pay for additional principals, classrooms. An additional one more year of schooling can do the following:

1. Build better classrooms than what passes as classrooms today
2. Buy modern equipment necessary to teach kids modern education
3. Train modern professional teachers who can teach creative studies
4. Hire science teachers abroad
5. The states and the local government will managed all public schools from Pre-k to universities. The federal, states and local government will jointly fund education.
6. Launch pilot programs for twenty-first-century educational system
7. Give every child free universal education

Every child from low income families will receive free education from Pre-k to high school, they also will receive free breakfast and lunch every day they attend school. University students will receive government grants and federal granted loan as well scholarships to obtain education without suffering. Universities and colleges need money to run better institutions.

Change Some University Degree Standards

For students to attain a modern standard of education, I think that the current way university courses and majors are structured can be upgraded to meet the international standard course like the following:

1. Medicine students who want to study this course should first and foremost complete a four-year-degree program in any science field before proceeding to study medicine.
2. Pharmacy requires BSc degree in any science field before proceeding to study pharmacy.
3. Law requires a BSc degree in liberal arts studies before proceeding to study law.
4. Engineering requires a BSc degree in computer science before proceeding to study engineering.

The National Youth Service Corps to Be Eliminated

NYSC, the National Youth Service Corps was a well-intentioned program that was started by General Yakubu Gowon after the Nigerian Civil War ended as a means of reconciliations among Nigerians slated to champion by the youths. Initially the program worked very well, and the newly minted university graduates were happy and proud to serve their country. The early administrators of the program did well managing it. It was assumed that the Nigerian Pandora's box was first opened in 1975 after the overthrow of Gowon government. The National Youths Services Corp was damaged when it became enmeshed into briber and corruptions after few years of existence. That single mistake destroyed the nation's robust economic future to date.

By 1980 the economic fallout had affected the normal functioning of the Youth Service Corps, and the youth interest in the service began to wane. Bribery and corruption took over where some Youth Corpers bribed officials to be assigned to places of their choice or to even skip serving at all. Today, this organization stinks and needs to be done with. No more National Youth Service. In the future, youths can be trained as military reserves or trained as National Guard reserves to be under the state governors. The best way to deal with this problem is for the government to investigate and set up a hearing where Nigerians and former Youth Corps will able to give testimony about the current state of this youth program. Doing this will enable the federal government to decide the fate and the future of the Youth Service. The government can save billions of naira wasted every year to run a criminal empire called the National Youth Service. This money saved should be used to create jobs for these youths, who after completing the service, never find a job.

The Health Care Reforms

The adage says that a healthy people is a healthy nation. After the independence, the nation benefitted from a well-established health care system left by the colonial masters, but not until 1976, when a ban on importation seriously affected the health care system because they no longer were able to import needed hospital equipment.

Foreign doctors left in droves. Today leaders pay little or no attention to health care for the masses because they use state funds to seek better health care for themselves and their families for free.

Today, children with only high school diplomas are rushed through medical schools run with inadequate medical resources to train them. The problems of the nation's health care system were identified by a former health minister, Dr. Ransome Kuti. However, he applied Band-Aid solutions to the problems when he ordered untrained and inexperienced auxiliary nurses to take over health care centers in the nation. Today, many of them still front as nurses and doctors with power to treat patients, prescribe and administer medications, give injections, deliver babies, and own private pharmacies without license. Today, these unqualified, uneducated, and untrained auxiliary nurses still control health care centers in the nation because they are meant for the masses. The government, doctors, and nurses are not raising an eyebrow even when they know that their noble profession is being murdered by untrained medical personals.

Wonders, they say, will never end in Nigeria. How can a group of people who have never received any sort of medical training now stage a battle with registered nurses for the control of professional medical delivery in the nation? The health care centers have no single doctor working there or even paying a visit once in a while.

Majority of the doctors do not want to work for government hospitals but instead opt to find and run one-room, one-doctor clinics all over the country in order to rip off their fellow citizens in the name of private medical practice. They theorize that opening their own clinics is the quickest way to get rich overnight instead of caring for people. In recent memory, in the name of tribalism, the nation has been dotted with teaching hospitals in every nook and corner of the country. These teaching hospitals do not meet the standard litmus test a teaching hospital in other places in the world have. Why should the federal government get involved in building underfunded teaching hospitals all over the nation?

The reasons behind building these teaching hospitals are not meant to address hospital shortages or neither to bring efficiency. But the simple reason is nothing but tribalism and corruption. It is a case where doctors from various tribes want to head a teaching hospital in their state of origin. These doctors do not care if there is enough fund or manpower to run these megainstitutions. If you happen to fall sick, you are most likely to die in the care of these teaching hospitals or private-run hospitals because of lack of equipment.

Today, many sick people refuse to go to hospitals but rather choose to patronize the alternative voodoo doctors to help them cure their ailments.

Teaching hospitals should be reformed and downsized and turned over to the private sector. The federal government and even state governments will not own or run teaching hospitals and other hospitals. But they can fund research with any of the private university teaching hospitals. The so-called federal government general hospitals will be turned over to the local governments and the private sector.

The time has come when all the auxiliary nurses will be banned from working in the hospitals and clinics. All health care centers in the country should be upgraded to full-fledged hospitals and clinics and be placed under the newly created states, cities, counties, suburbs, and boroughs jointly funded by both federal governments and state governments. All of the hospitals must be staffed with doctors, registered nurses, and other health care professionals and hospital administrators and office staffs.

Over 90 percent of private hospitals and clinics should be shut down until after reforms to start again if they meet the standard benchmark to be set for operating new hospitals. Private hospital and clinic developers must be able to show proof that they have credit and cash of not less than one billion naira to start a new hospital and clinic. The federal government should set up board of inquiries to probe all the teaching hospitals and private hospitals and clinics. It is better to have just few working private and teaching hospitals than have thousands of nonworking hospitals and clinics.

In 1996 I visited Nigerian I fell sick. The illness was such a serious one that I was losing weight, dehydrated, as well as urinating frequently. To found out the problem I went and took blood test. However, the problem was not solved because the blood test result indicated that nothing was wrong with me. Then I went to the doctor he told me that I am suffering from malaria parasite and gave me an injection and pills and sent me home. When I got home I collapsed and about to die. It was early in the morning the next day that I was rush to the hospital and after another blood test that is when it was found out that I am suffering from type 2 diabetes and my blood sugar level was as high as 850 to 1000 counts. And a doctor already told me that I had malaria instead diabetes and then gave me malaria injection. A kind of a death sentence.

Pharmacy Owners

It is a nation where pharmacies are owned by uneducated, untrained people who also prescribe drugs to their patients while the doctors look on. The Nigerian pharmacist sells their license to this untrained illegal drug paddlers to cover them up. Corruption has hit the health care delivery very hard. The system needs reforms to outlaw those who are not licensed to handle drugs to stop them. Pharmacists who illegally trade their license with money to protect these illegal drug sellers should be sanctioned and heavily fined and given jail term. The government should endeavor to provide health care for all

The Proliferations of DNA Centers

They are too many DNA centers all over the country and many of them operates under unsanitary conditions. Many of them may not be qualify to run these centers, and many are operated illegally. The government should cut down on these centers to about ninety five level allowing only five percent to operate until after reforms.

Nigerian Constitution and State and City Statutes and Penal Codes

For the sake of Nigerians, the current constitution should be reexamined and publicly debated to make sure that the rights of every citizen are guaranteed. The constitution should be framed on the basis of the nation's background and environment as a secular nation, a nation where no religion will be permitted to rule or have a separate court, a constitution that will lay emphasis on the adversary legal system under common law as the nation's legal system only, that all Nigerians, no matter their religious beliefs, no matter what states they are born or come from, are one and free to live with full rights as legal citizens of any state and local government where they call their home, that all Nigerians are created equally. The use of *state of origins* must be outlawed in the constitution. But for the purpose of census and statistics, dialect question can be asked to keep records of demographics in terms of getting a job, benefits programs. To protect citizens against all forms of discrimination, a civil rights law should be enacted and passed. Tort laws should also be passed. Freedom of speech and freedom of press laws must be passed because it will help the nation to grow up.

At least fifty wise men and women should be selected to review the constitution. To pick the fifty constitutional review members, balloting should be use. Nigerians should be given the opportunity to exercise their fundamental rights to vote and choose who they believe will best represent their interest and that of the nation. The judicial system is broken and is in need of top to down reforms.

Jobs, Jobs, and Jobs

Jobs cannot be created without reforms. In fact, my paper has offered a road map to the shortest and the longest way to fix Nigeria. What Nigerians needed most today are jobs and jobs! The government must give jobs creation the nation the highest priority. Nigerians need a living wage jobs now! This can be achieved as big milestone if tribalism, nepotism, favoritism, and corruption will not stand in the way of doing this. This milestone can be as well accomplished if the government agrees not to hide any secret on the state of the nation economy barometer, politics, and social dysfunctionality. It can also be possible if they agree to work with trusted international communities to reform the nation's economy.

How to Create Twenty Million Jobs in Five Years and Additional Four Million Jobs Every Year

The priority in the country today is putting Nigerians back to work after more than forty years of experiencing the worst unemployment situation in the history of the country as a result of public decrees by the politicians and the military leaders. To achieve these goals, the government should call out for joint effort by all citizens since everyone desires a better a life.

The nation's human capital, natural resources should be activated and put in full use. The nation should seriously consider seeking for international allies as partners in progress. Allies that would agree to enter into trade agreement with the nation would bring in much needed technology. The nation should be prepared to end its foreign diplomatic marriage between her and the so-called African Nonally Movement, it is about time the federal government of Nigeria decides whom they want to be their friends, allies and trading partners around the globe for the sake of its people.

To begin the step-by-step journey of putting Nigerians back to work, It is about time the government should think twice before over regulating the economy that is always counterproductive to economic growth that favor only the few. These unproductive economic regulations have been tried for over forty years and have not worked. Instead, they ended up setting the nation's economic development backwards. These counterproductive public policies killed jobs and businesses. In this era of world global economy, the nation should strive to become a partner, which should be one of the reasons for reforms.

For a start, the nation's leaders should be willing to seek for trade partners around the globe and enter into comprehensive trade agreements with such trusted allies. The nation should look up to the West, especially America and Britain, to form economic allies. Many people in Africa believe that the world economic globalization is another form of globalization and slavery introduced by the West to steal from the poor countries. My friend, do not be afraid because the world has gotten wiser. A new market economy that will emphasize on private sector economic empowerment for large, medium, and small businesses with operating data should be pursued as a new way of doing business in the nation. The private sector economy has been in the doldrums for forty years and cannot be rebuilt by creating more frivolous government ministries after frivolous government ministries and agencies that are only good for paying overhead cost. This money can be invested to develop the private sector economy.

The reformers must make sure that in the future, businesses and individuals should be able to obtain loans and credits to help them grow their businesses to create jobs. It is something that is not happening in the country, except if you are among the privileged few. Reforms' goals should be to undo the current system that has been practiced for years without good result. Should the nation embark on carrying out serious top-to-bottom reforms, they will look forward to having the Paris Club forgive the nation's debts and then once again spur international business investors to come to the nation to start investing again, which will help to create millions of jobs for Nigerians.

Economic Recovering

NEPA, the National Electric Power Authority, was illegally sold behind the backs of Nigerians and should be revoked. After its revocation by the federal government, it should be passed over to the states, cities, suburbs, and counties to find worthy international investors to enter into a contract agreement with them to take over electric supply. The federal government will no longer be allowed to waste money in the name of getting physically involved in electricity supply because it has been on it for more than fifty years but failed. Every single budget allocation for the supply of electricity was stolen.

The government's claim to have privatized the national electric power project was a trick because after that, the government continued to fund it. If government had sold the power supply to the private sector, giving them 100 percent control of electric power supply, why did they continue to pump billions of dollars into it? The privatization of this industry and the government's continued involvement calls for inquiries. The federal government allocating billions of dollars annually to the private owners is quite suspicious. The government should publish the names of these private owners.

Despite the billions of dollars of allocation, the power supply become worse, and power failures became endemic. These private owners collect trillions of naira worth of electric bills from Nigerians annually without supplying them light. Reforms must make sure that no government will be allowed to be physically involved in power supply in the nation. It must be in the hands of the private investors who have the ability, finances, and technology to supply the nation with twenty-four-hour electricity.

Telecommunications

Assuminng privatization was done in a truthful and honest manners its architects would have first reformed the country. The idea to Auction entities like the National Telecommunication company, Refineries, Oil wells, the National electricity Power Authority and the prime real-estates among others to few rich Nigerians men, women and their surrogates financiers backfired because they did not possessed the ability to keep these entities or use them to create jobs. Many of them ended up abandoned, and many of them did not meet the expectations that were required of them.

It is sad to say that President Obasanjo used his purported privatization to auction away the Nigerian Telecommunication company and other big name corporations to few Nigerians whom he knows very well that they lack the financial and technological ability to manage and run these mega- companies efficiently. Today these corporations are not meeting their expectations of providing better services to the people. The owners use it to rip off Nigerians by collecting monthly bills for services that was never rendered and never will be rendering any better service.

The common complaints you hear from Nigerians is network problems after network problems. The government's purported privatization of the telecommunication industry was a farce. Privatization was tainted with corruption. The initiators sold this corporation to themselves, families, and friends. Today they make billions of dollars off Nigerians without providing excellent communication network services. This is an important sector of the economy that should face serious reforms because of its potential to create thousands of high-tech jobs and bring the much needed computer technology to the nation. A reputable new international wireless company should be given the contract to take charge of telecommunication network operations after reviewing the performance of its current owners.

In fact, if the federal government is serious about creating jobs, jobs, jobs, jobs, and jobs, the following actions are required to be taken:

1. The economic embargoes or ban on the importation of goods decreed more than forty years ago, which caused the economy to crash and brought down a once progressive economy, should be lifted.
2. The indigenization decrees enacted during the Gowon government should be revoked. Naturalizations and privatizations during Obasanjo's government should be revoked and completely undone.
3. All the affected companies, such as UAC, UTC, John Holt, Kingsway Stores, Leventis Stores and Levant's Motors Ltd., Barclays Bank, Standard Bank, Bank of America, all the international businesses that were seized or forced to pull out of the country, should be returned to its original owners. In an effort to give back the seized international businesses to its original owners, the federal government should charge each of these former business owners to pay just one penny to recover their businesses.

No individual should be allowed to reap where he or she did not sow; therefore, any Nigerian who was given or pretended to have purchased these businesses should surrender these businesses back to their original and rightful owners. Once they pay the amount of one penny to the federal government, they should be able to recover their businesses without hassle. Also to be surrendered are empty lands, offices, empty buildings, banks; the places where they previously ran their businesses throughout the country before the seizures should be relinquished no matter what the land or buildings is being used for today. By accepting one penny and returning them, it will definitely translate into billions and billions of dollars of new investments that may create millions of jobs for Nigerians as well as give the nation access to modern technologies.

Obasanjo's privatizations and sales of the people's prime real estates to few rich Nigerian, families, friends, and cronies should be revoked and investigated. The actions of Obasanjo towards his people were quite undemocratic. No one would be against privatization if reforms had taken place first and the reasons for it was to create jobs and a better life for the people.

The privatization effort under Obasanjo's administration was dubious from start to finish because his terming, rush, and the undemocratic way, style, and manner it was carried out. He auctioned the nation's most prime real estates and corporations to families and friends and top government officials through the use of foreign surrogates who provided the funds. These businesses were auctioned for pennies to those who lacked the technical knowledge and finances to run them. The privatizations merit investigations, probing, and revocations. This was the same administration that started as far back as 1976 to nationalize foreign-owned businesses, and in 1999 he once again imposed himself on Nigerians as president and created another economic havoc for the nation. His public policy and decrees killed well-established businesses and jobs and increased poverty and hunger. Perhaps he didn't know how to use his public policy to increase productivity and create jobs and a better life for the people.

Auctioned Items

The Nigerian refineries, the cement companies, steel mills, refineries, industries, NEPA, the most expensive real estates in the nation in the most expensive prime areas of the nation including other Nigerian properties were auctioned to families and friends and top government officials during Obasanjo's administration, and it should be held accountable for deceiving Nigerians.

The entire so-called privatization should be revoked, undone, and returned back to Nigerian people to determine the best way to deal with it.

The president and his lady finance minister know fully well that the auction beneficiaries do not possess the mental ability, financial ability, technical ability, and the management ability to run and manage these megacorporations. Instead, these buyers misused the opportunity to use it to increase productivity and create jobs for Nigerians.

In all account privatization was a major blow to the economy because it was ill- intended from start to finish. Billions and billions of dollars was stolen in the name of privatizations and it merits government probe.

The money used to buy out these corporations and real-estates was provided by foreign surrogate to Nigerian looters who fronted as the real buyers. These stolen properties are operated with the names of these looters. They proceeded to transfer billions of dollars of their ill-gotten wealth to their foreign bank accounts while Nigerians suffered unemployment and untold hardships. They collect billions of dollars of monthly bills from helpless Nigerians without rendering services of any type. The only justification for privatization was to enrich families, friends, and surrogates.

The time for accountability is due, and Nigerians cannot wait to see it happen. Leaders, whether past or current, should be held accountable for their deeds during their time in office and should be compelled to lender an account of their stewardship to the people. This is a nation where leaders enjoy exploiting the ignorance of the masses on what government should be or should not be.

Nigerians should cast their blame on the few privileged elites who know the bad things going in the country but shut up their mouths after they are bribed. They are part of the problems the nation is facing today.

Obasanjo and his finance minister did not require any lecture to know the consequentiality of his naturalization of foreign businesses in the seventies. He should have been reminded that his economic decrees were a major contributing factor that brought down an advancing, progressive, forward-looking economy for years. Because of these past failures, he should have proceeded with caution by first initiating comprehensive reforms. His first consideration was to determine if returning these seized and failed businesses to their former owners would have been more helpful to the economy. It was him and his predecessor that seized these businesses in the seventies, so he stood the better chance to revoke and undo the seizures and return them to their rightful owners, which would have helped to restart the failed economy. Secondly, he should have known that the business seizures were the primary cause of Nigerian failed state. He should have had the courage to return these businesses to the owners to redevelop them as measure to create jobs and opportunities for Nigerians. The president missed the best opportunity he had to jump-start the economy when he embarked on another destructive policy by using privatization as an excuse to shut down the economy again.

Nigerian will welcome it, if president Obasanjo and his finance minister can tell the country the reasons behind privatization before reforms. It would also be nice as well if they will revealed the amount of money realized from these sales and what it was use for? Despite privatization the country continue to suffer from endemic power supply, fuel shortages, lack of clean water and unemployment among other things.

He loves to take advantage of the ignorance of the masses and fools them by pretending that he cares for them. This is a man who refuses to believe that his eccentric economic decrees crushed the nation's economy and sent millions and millions of Nigerians to the unemployment market and created massive poverty and criminal enterprises in the nation, causing both local and foreign businesses to fall down on their faces.

For more than forty years the Nigerians people were made to suffer the fall out of the bad economic and social policies created by their self-appointed leaders. Were his decrees based on national interest or on his selfish personal interests? No one else can answer this question but him. Today, many Nigerians exist on one dollar per day. How could this happen in an oil-rich nation? Enough is enough. It is time for a change.

If Nigeria's past and current leaders could be comfortable enough to admit that the nation is a failed state because of their past economic decrees and public policies, it could help the nation to heal and think about a better way to start economic recovery. Forty years of failures is enough for the government to turn the table and begin anew.

Does anyone believe that only a nation's domestic products will be enough to propel its economic growth without trading with other nations? The adage says, "A tree cannot make a forest." The nation needs friends and allies. It is time to join forces with the rest of the world for the sake of the nation's economic development.

Potential Allies

The United States of America, Great Britain, and the European Union should be considered as the nation's centerpiece of its future foreign policy to secure trade agreement with these nations that will help to spur economic development and create jobs for Nigerians.

Can anyone imagine the way this nation could be transformed into a technological state in few years if it formed a collective partnership with international allies with some trusted nations? The international allies will be the ones the nation will like to enter into trade agreement with.

The Marshall Plan is needed to fix and build a new and better Nigeria. The nation needs to train and nurture a brand-new set of young, talented, creative, skilled, and progressive men and women with respect to ethics to assume the responsibility of rebuilding the nation and effecting the critically needed reforms. It will be expected that after reforms are completed, businesses like Microsoft, IBM, Google, Facebook, Yahoo, YouTube, Amazon, eBay, Twitter, Instagram, just to name a few, will no doubt like to invest in Nigeria, businesses that can create thousands of high-tech jobs that pay very well in addition to bringing the much needed technology and even help to light the nation twenty-four hours a day.

The government may grant working visas to foreign talented, creative, skilled young entrepreneurs to come to Nigeria to work and establish businesses. These people can be a big benefit in growing the economy.

Industries

Next is the industrial manufacturing enterprises that could be invited from overseas. This sector could not only create thousands of jobs but also will help the nation to produce domestic products for consumption and export finished goods around the world.

Manufacturing companies such as Chrysler, Ford Motors, GM, Toyota, Honda Motor, Mercedes, BMW, General Electric, and many others may be interested to come to manufacture vehicles here. If they do accept to come here, they should be allowed to purchase and rebuild the Nigerian steel industries for their use and export. They will play a big role to help fix the nation's electricity.

Other businesses such as fast-food companies, megasupermarkets, Macy's stores, J. C. Penny, H&M, Old Navy, AT&T, Sony, movie theaters and moviemakers, casinos, hotels, Wal-Mart Stores, Kingsway Stores may be interested to establish their businesses here if allowed. Many formerly expelled businesses may like to come back if business conditions are changed.

All the formally seized international banks should be returned to their rightful owners by the government and charge them just one penny for them to get their businesses back because in the end, it will translate into trillions of dollars of business investments and millions of jobs. Banks to be returned to their owners are Standard Bank, now called First Bank; Bank of America, now called Savanah Bank but may be out of business now; Barclay's Bank, now called Union Bank; and UBA.

Interested new foreign banks should be given a free pass to establish here. Of course, if the nation is interested in growing the economy and wants to stabilize its economy, they should allow foreign banks to come in because they will be the ones to finance business in the amount of billions of dollars. Banks like HSBC, Banco Santander, Chase Bank, Citibank, Bank of America, and so on and so forth could be given access to establish here. Their major roles will be to attract foreign investors like Fortune 500 companies to our shores. These banks are capable to grant loans and credit to businesses that will grow the economy. It is something that the local banks are not doing today.

Should not be considered a shame to bring into the country some well-known foreign real-estates developers to help construct modern cities as the nation begin a new era. Armed with a newly minted Marshall Plan, states, cities, counties, and suburbs including water, electricity, roads, bridges, schools, hospitals, offices, modern underground drainage system, passenger railroads, mass transport systems, and so on will be designed and built. As soon as reforms are completed, constructions will start. To achieve these goals, the government will have to set up a special fund for the construction projects, giving them access to bank credit and loans. It will be constructions, constructions, constructions, constructions, and constructions in the nation for a feasible future. The nation should go back to commercial farming, which is an area where another thousands of jobs can be created.

After reforms when ethics standards might have been established, American anthropologist scientists should be invited and be given the contracts to bring in their high-tech equipment in addition to their experience and expertise in locating and cataloguing these mineral deposits with honesty.

Americans, Britons, and Italians are very good in construction and should be made partners. The nation should not lose sight that Britain still considers them as their baby and will be more than willing to help Nigeria to recover economically if they allowed them. For any of these proposals to take shape, the nation should find willing foreign allies. Having some friendly and trustworthy allies will pay dividends for the nation's future economic developments.

Nigeria can position itself to take lead command in controlling an eight-hundred-million-consumers market in the African continent that has largely been overlooked for years because of wars, poverty, and diseases that have consumed the continent since after gaining independence. Because of the nation's oil wealth along with its rich human capital, Nigeria would stand a better chance to control this market if their leaders can swallow their pride and seek friendship with trusted international allies that can enter into trade agreement with the nation.

These new allies are the ones that can help the nation to rebuild their critical infrastructures to bring back jobs as well as build manufacturing companies of all types that will make Nigeria an international goods exporter in the near future. And this is the way Nigeria can take the command lead to control more than eight hundred million consumers in the market in the continental African nations and as well as exporting their finished products to other parts of the world stamped with Nigerian export visa. If the federal government should stop running a failed state and stop throwing the nation's money down the pit, the nation can be fixed. They have run a government that has never worked for the people since attaining independence.

Television and Radio Houses

The federal-government owned television stations and radio stations and other mass media outlets should be dismantled and be made 100 percent private-sector enterprises. This too will create thousands of good-paying jobs for Nigerians and will help to stop the government from interfering with free speech and freedom of press in the country. What if the nation can attract icons like Oprah Winfrey Television and Radio and Oprah Winfrey University?

I have deliberately omitted including the oil sector as a new job creator because it has been established but needs major reforms. The Nigerian government should understand that the country cannot continue to pin its hope on oil as a major source of revenue, which account for about 98 percent of the national revenue that the government only spends to pay overhead cost, and whatever is left is stolen, and nothing is left to develop the nation.

New Revenue Sources

The time has come when the government has to come up with another source of earning revenue rather than betting the nation's future only on oil dependence. You can see in recent months the price of oil has been nose-diving. If it continues like this, it will spell an economic doom for the nation. Again, many nations have recently been discovering oil. America even has more oil wells than Nigeria. What if they decide to go full swing and begin to tap their oil wells? Also, many nations are now discovering alternative energy sources. Other nations are planning to use hydraulic gas fracking for energy sources.

Nothing to Show for Oil Wealth

Should be considered a letdown that for more than half-century this country have earned billions and billions of dollars from selling oil there is absolutely nothing tangibles to show for it?An oil producing nation that suffers from endemic fuel scarcity that has become a curse.

The time has come for Nigerians to ask those who led them for more than half a century one question: Where is our oil money? Nigerians want an answer to this question. Based on this question, it has become very necessary to reform and fix Nigeria to benefit everyone. It is time to uproot, destroy, and rebuild bigger, greater, better, and stronger for generations of Nigerians to come. It is time to send these thieving bums packing. It is time to shake the foundation of this country and rebuild it with the greatest foundations for generations to come.

Nigeria/China

Nigerians could trade with China on official capacity only, which means that there will be a trade agreement between the two nations. Chinese businessmen and businesswomen will not be allowed to come to Nigeria to bribe government officials to gain favor above others or connive with some dubious Nigerian businessmen and businesswomen to rip off the people by selling fake goods. Nigerian trade agreement with China will be based on products to be manufactured in Nigeria and marked with Made in Nigeria that will be exported back to China and other nations. China cannot solve the current economic woes in the nation, but they cannot be dismissed if they play well. There have been rumors about contacts worth of billions dollars given to some Chinese businessmen that were never executed after collecting money from the government.

Egregious Nigerian Budgets

You are going to be frighten if you ever venture to read this country's budgets you will be shock if you see the way and manner the architects of these budgets systematically write budgets that are filled with ghost workers and ghost contractors. The finance minister and the Director General write the budgets, appropriate and award the contracts to individuals who are connected to them before the budgets become law. For example I found that a winter coat was purchased for government official for thousands of dollars a coat that would had cost between $100.00 -$200.00 dollars but was purchased at the cost of about $4000.00 dollars very appalling, in deed. Contracts was awarded for the constructions of one class room, two class room class room to tunes of millions naira. This is just a tip of the icebeg. The budgets are atrocious and awful to read but it be read, however. The time has ripe for the government to audit and probe budgets from 1999-2015 so that the budgets Pandora box can be open for the public to see. The culprits must be held accountable.

The government should restore paying families with foreign currency amount their wards sent to them with Western Union. The alternative foreign exchange market is legal so no law is violated if they are paid in foreign currency. Recipients loses so much money if banks pay them with local currency.

The Central Bank of Nigeria is responsible in inventing outlandish after outlandish monetary policies that continue to ruin the economy for over forty years now. Added to the commercial bank that are just lame ducks they contribute nothing to grow the economy because they work only for their pockets. Ever since Clement Isong the former governor of Central bank of Nigeria retired the bank has never been the same again. Most of the stolen oil money find their way out of the country with Central bank approvals, the bank is house of fraud. It is time to probe and reform the Central bank of Nigeria. After reforms the next wave of business enterprises will be start-up and franchises

Despite the failures of their economic policies that left the nation a "Failed States for more thirty years now they "remain inert displaying a neglect and insouciance that borders on denial"

I sincerely appeal to rich nations around the world to rescue and help to restore the shattered African nations economic for the sake of the suffering masses. African nations is an earthquake waiting to erupt if this problems are not immediately address. They need foods, jobs, jobs and jobs and good education that will make them to think creatively. The world wouldn't like to create another terrorist hub because these people are really tied and angry with their leaders for been abandoned and forgotten for years. However, Africans are not asking for handouts just to help them rebuild their economies in order to create a better life for everyone

Economic Stabilization Claims

The government's claim of stabilizing the economy and bringing down the runaway foreign exchange and hyperinflation appears to be a myth. Forty years after their insane public decrees crushed the economy and ended the nation's employment opportunities and ended a once-robust middle class, they continued doing the same thing over and over without a different result. Today the entire federation of Nigeria has only 2,001 companies and no Fortune 500 companies for a population of 200 million people. Majority of these companies are concentrated in Lagos and Abuja. Many of the states do not have a single company; don't even count the local government areas throughout the federation because it is empty. Is it the way to build a progressive society?

Compare that to New York City; the city alone harbors more than one million companies for just seven million of New York City residents, which does not include the New York State or the entire United States of America but just one city in America. Nigeria has a long way to go, but to have as many companies as possible is within its reach if it does the right thing of forming allies with some trusted nations in the world. This nation is losing its potentials on a daily basis to other nations due to hardships. Talents, skills, and creativity are thrown to the dogs because they are no longer required in the nation to succeed in life.

Moving forward, Nigerians should demand the federal government to release all the white papers pertaining to indigenization, naturalization, and privatizations and the names of its beneficiaries and the amount they paid for them. Nigerians should demand as well the release of all the white papers pertaining to Abuja's development projects and the names and owners of all the luxurious houses, plazas, hotels, and lands in Abuja Town. Who are the owners and what were their jobs and income before they acquired these properties because Nigerians are ready to search and to recover their stolen oil wealth? Also, the white papers pertaining to Otta farms should be released so that Nigerians may see it to learn who is the rightful owner, whether it is owned by President Obasanjo or Nigerians. They will also like to know the ways and manner of the farm acquisitions and where the money came from.

All former military decrees are subject to revocation because they were undemocratic and unjust laws, making it unacceptable to Nigerians. Nigerian people want accountability on the whereabouts of their oil wealth Where is the Nigerian oil wealth? Please, we the people of Nigeria are asking the Nigerian leaders both past and present to tell the people where they kept the oil money. Where is the people's oil wealth? This question will continue to be asked until someone gives Nigerians an answer. Nigerians are appealing to the international community to help to find this stolen wealth. Individuals and governments around the world who know where the people's stolen wealth is hidden, we appeal for your help to return the loot for the sake of the innocent suffering masses!

It is time for Nigerian authorities to bury their pride and agree to form an alliance with America, Great Britain, European Union, and as far back as Australia and others, and if it is achieved, then the nations will be ready for business. They should make an effort to secure a tight, trusted friendship with these nations, which may lead to trade agreements.

As part of the trade agreement, the Nigerian authorities can ask these nations to send graduate students from these Ivy League universities such as Harvard, MIT, Warton, Kellogg, Yale, Princeton, Stanford, Columbia, Oxford, Duke, and so on from all fields to work with their counterparts in Nigeria to help plan a new republic. Part of their assignment is to produce a Marshall Plan for the nation and then serve as expert advisers.

The American Peace Corps can be requested to help out in revising the educational system as well as teach in schools up to university level and also help to recommend a new, modern standard of learning, a modern standard type of classrooms, buildings, equipment, technology needed to impart high-quality education to Nigerian children. The nation could accept the support from these nations and its institutions of higher learning; they will certainly do a great and a wonderful job of designing a brand-new progressive society for all. Millions of jobs will be created. And they will quickly help the country to go high-tech. This is not about neocolonialism but rather business and partnership and friendships for the good of the nations involved.

Laws and security will be top issues. Business owners want to be secure both in person and for their businesses and to obey the law of the land. The government should pass law that will grant foreign investors right to do business in the country without government interference on how they conduct their businesses as long as they obey the law of the land and maintain fairness.

They are free to hire employees from their home countries because this nation too needs a diversity of talents, skills, and creativity to move the nation forward. Nigerians and people around the world can work and live together. They will be no quota for any demographics, rather competence, talent, skills, and creativity will be the determining factors for anyone to be hired.

Government should grant honorable citizenships and permanent residence to foreign business owners to give them assurance that they own their businesses for life and as long as they are in business in Nigeria. No Nigerian, no matter how pious or powerful he or she may be, can initiate the seizure of any foreign business. A law to guard foreign businesses against government interference or abuse should be written and passed. A friendly and conducive environment must be provided. The federal government cannot dictate for companies where to site their businesses after they ink trade agreements with a nation or nations. It must be 100 percent private sector businesses that will be better handled at local government level instead of on the federal government level in order to avoid it becoming another excuse for bribery and corruption. The federal government and the local government should provide low-tax incentive to attract businesses. Affordable lands and mortgages should also be considered for businesses. To crown it, civil rights laws and its impact theories should be passed.

Crime control and prevention is a must to attract foreign businesses. They must be protected in person as well as their businesses to prove to it is secure, conducive, and safe as a good business environment, which all businesses expect whether domestic or foreign. Communities should be targeted for crime control and prevention if evidence of criminal activities exist in any area of the community. Although terror and terrorists attacks now affect almost every nation in the world. Nigeria as well is affected with terrorists' menace and has been battling to defeat Boko Haram. Having said this, Boko Haram's illegal intrusion into the affairs of Nigerian people's lives would not be enough reason for businesses to reject doing business with Nigeria because right now Nigerian people need jobs. Terrorism has become a global issue and global cancer that needs effort from all nations around the world as well as the effort and hard work of good citizens in the world to defeat them.

Alternative Means of Revenue

The time has come when the government will start to think about other sources of earning revenue. Oil as a major revenue earner can be now kept in the second burner. The country has large amounts of mineral deposits and other forms of natural resources that have not been officially tapped, except the ones that are stolen through the back door by some dubious foreign businessmen who become billionaires with it. These foreign businessmen who also come from some third world country are well known in the country. This time around they will be exposed. Because this venture requires high-tech equipment to discover and tap, the country should seek for reputable businessmen and businesswomen from the country that the nation plans to enter into trade agreement with.

The federal government, states, cities, counties, and suburbs should write a new tax code to collect corporate tax, income taxes, payroll taxes, sale taxes, property taxes, and so on. Certain luxury goods such as cars, tires, wines, fuel should be taxed. This new form of revenue generator can earn the country more money than it gets from oil. But then millions and millions of jobs must be created.

Tax Law and Collection

The legislative body should pass a law that will mandate every citizen and noncitizen to file their business taxes, corporate taxes, payroll taxes, individual income taxes, small business taxes, self-employed personal income taxes, property taxes, and oil and gas taxes. It should be mandatory that every citizen and noncitizen should file their tax returns with the Federal Internal Revenue Services every year beginning from the month of February to May. Special professional tax preparers will be trained and licensed to help tax filers to file their taxes. While some will be free for low-income tax returns, others will have to pay fees for their services. Such fees will be determined by the government. The emphasis on job creations must be placed on the doorstep of private sector economy if the government is serious on revising its current method of revenue-generating sources based solely on relying on oil. None of these proposals will work if ethics, transparency, and honesty are not restored in government and the people themselves. Strong laws should be made to guide against abuse. Taxing Nigerians does not mean overkill or overtaxing businesses because doing so will defeat the intended purpose. Tax incentives must be given to businesses to help them operate with profit. All federal, state, and local taxes must be filed and returned with the Federal Internal Revenue Services. To achieve this goal, the nation must be prepared to go full throttle into embracing technology.

National Assets Declarations

The government should make it a mandatory requirements for every Nigerian whether rich or poor to file their annual income taxes returns from February to May every year. Also to be file is business taxes both small businesses and corporate.

Meeting this national obligation should be made mandatory for everyone rich or poor. Everyone is to declare his or her assets every once in a year. It is called assets declaration. Anyone who is declaring his or her assets should list their name, age, residential address, nature of job, income amount, value of landed properties, and stock. The individual should also state the time the day, month, and year it was acquired and type of work he or she had during that period. To be included are cash at hand and in the bank and landed properties, and stocks acquired at home and abroad must be reported.

There will be no exceptions from this law, beginning from the president of the nation, all former heads of state, all former governors and current ones, all former government and private business top officials, all current ministers and former ministers and members, national and state lawmakers, and from the richest to the poorest, all must obey this law. The purpose of this law will be a way to restore transparency, ethics, accountability, and honesty in the government and in the country as a whole that will form a major part of the reforms and a way to fix and save the nation's finances from being stolen anymore. The assets declarations will be in force for a foreseeable future until the country is able to minimize bribery, corruption, and mismanagement. Among those who had the rare opportunity to rule this country none of them will be proud of the ugly state of the country today.

Social Security Number

For the reforms to be effective and to benefit Nigerians, every Nigerian citizen must have a security number from the time of his or her birth. Whether old or young must have this number in order to be able to receive government benefits and file taxes, file their assets declarations, register their children in schools, go to hospitals, do banking, and rent or buy a house or land and get a job. In the past, the country had one called the national provident fund, where Nigerian workers and employers contributed money to the fund against retirement. But due to mismanagement and embezzlement, it was laid to rest. Nigerian workers lost all their savings. Up to date, no one has told Nigerian workers what happened to their savings paid into the national provident fund. No one has been held accountable. The national security number is mandatory for everyone living in Nigeria.

A few years ago the federal government started the national identification program but ended in a mess according to the way Nigerian government officials handled the people's business as if it does not matter. It ended in bribery and corruption, making some Nigerians lucky enough to get the federal identity and majority of others not lucky enough to get the federal identity cards. For a reminder to the federal government, the issuance of the national security identity cards programs is not a police or civil defense job.

Instead the federal government will create an agency that will be called the Federal Social Security Administration, which will hire and train employees to be entirely responsible to run the organization, which will include workers' and employers' contributions as retirement savings. They will be responsible to issue new national identity cards to Nigerians and to replace the old or lost ones. Because it is a case-sensitive project, it must be under federal control to avoid duplication and fraud. The offices of the national identity cards should be spread throughout the federation in every state and every local government area. Every Nigerian must be issued with it in order to enable them to transact business in the country. Immigrants who are qualified will also be issued national identity cards.

Ethical Code of Conduct

This is a serious issue right now in the nation that the government needs to address through reforms. Government, businesses, and individuals lack ethical conduct when dealing with each other, hence institutionalization of fraud, bribery, and corruption in every nook and corner of the nation.

To make this possible, the federal government, state governments, and all local governments should pass rules and regulations that will mandate all government offices and businesses in the country to introduce customer's bill of rights. This means that all governmental offices and businesses that deal directly with the public where money and other essential services are involved must write their customer's bill of rights.

For example, police and citizens' bill of rights should include all the rights of an offender such as arrest and detention time, fees if any, the right to be given a lawyer if poor, right to remain silent, right not to be beaten or tortured, right to be fed while under arrest. The customer's and citizen's bill of rights will list all of customs tariffs, duties, and fees with full description of charges. Every information importer or exporter travelers are required to know must be disclosed in the bill of rights. Others are airport's bill of rights for departing and arriving passengers' services and fees if any must be disclosed by the Customs and Port Authority. To stop constant graft at the seaports and airports agencies operating here will be mandated to post customers' bills of rights that show its fees and charges. Agencies such as, Customs, Immigrations, Ports Authority, Airports Authority and clearing agents should keep this rule. The hard copy of the bills of right must always be given to customers when they use these facilities. All local government offices must write their citizen's bill of rights listing all their fees and charges. The nations education departments and all schools and universities of learning must write its parents'/student's bill of rights listing all fees as it pertains to each school federal and state and local that cover these fees. All federal and state office must write their citizen's bill of rights. Finally, all private businesses must as well write their customer's bill of rights by listing all services and fees. Written bill of rights should be handed over to citizens or customers each time they use any of these services for them to know their rights. This is an attempt to find solutions to the nation's institutionalization of bribery, fraud, and corruption in the country.

Probe the Leaders

As reforms proceeded the misdeeds of previous administrators should be probe to know who and who are responsible to what happened to this country and if they are found wanted they should be held accountable to prevent future occurrences. Members of congress and state governors should do so as well. All investigation and inquiries should be made public.

The Nigerian Customs

This organization has failed the nation time and time again. It is a heaven for bribery, fraud, and corruption. At least 99 percent of customs officials do not live on their monthly incomes. For the past forty years, after Nigerian leaders enacted antiquated backward economic decrees, Nigerian customs officials themselves alone personally pocketed billions of dollars' worth of government customs revenue. They are among the richest people in the nation. The only way to stop them from robbing the people will be to normalize the situation by the government lifting the trade embargoes put in place more than forty years ago. The department should be investigated and probed and downsized.

Of course, bribery, fraud, and corruption affect every single Nigerian. It is in a critical situation that something needs to be done. It is a merry-go-round. About eighty percent of Nigerians live above their means of income and this is a serious set-back to the nation's ability to advance its economic growth. It is a nation where almost everybody is equally guilty of the same offense.

The president and the members of the legislative bodies should enact and pass laws to help curb bribery, fraud, and corruption to some manageable level for the benefit of everyone.

Because of the re-introduction of [a] FORM M [b] Standard Organization of Nigeria Conformity Assessment Program. [SONCAP] [c] Pre-Arrival Assessment Report [PARR] is exact repeation of the 70s and 80s import policy that shatters the economy. It is a pity that this country only benefits from arm-chair technocrats who knows little or nothing about their country. They never leave their glass doors to venture into town to measure the health of the economy before making another counterproductive public policy that will affect millions of lives. This import policy is so counterproductive that the government is losing billions and billions of naira every day to customs officers, police officers, ports authority workers, importers and clearing agents without the government having any the clue. Most public policies may not work in a corrupt and polarized country like Nigeria. They did not understand the mental psych of Nigerians on how they perceive government public policy and that is the problem. Letter of credit should replace Form M, Soncap and Parr. The issue is that in order to solve this problem the following action are required to be taken, [1] This policy should be cancelled. [2] Government should lift the ban on imports only for new products, such as Cars, Trucks and Parts, Computers, food, Industrial Machineries, and so many others. The only imports that will remain ban is illegal Drugs and arms [3] Outlaw the imports of Junks, Used goods referred to as [TOKUBO] goods which will includes cars,trucks,parts,electronic computers, food, clothing, industrial equipment and so many others from entering into the country. The imports of Junks used goods are killing the economy. For example the nation's highways, streets and markets are filled with these junks goods brought home from Europe and other countries. It has become an eyesore and a disgrace to an oil rich nation, the nation is losing trillions of naira in customs revenue every year, its environmental effect is too much and there is no landfills or adequate recycle plants to take care of all these junks, the average life of cars, trucks brought into the country starts from 200 to more than 250 miles. Parts are just junks. Banning these type of goods from entering the country will help the process of stabilizing the economy and as well as strength the naira against the dollar and the pound sterling's.[4] The government should introduce the use of Letter of Credits for imports and exports. To solve the problem of bribery and corruption at our seaport and airport importers and exporters will open a letter of credit with their banks, if any importer or exporter is qualify he can obtain a loan and credit from the bank to purchase his goods, however, an importer or exporter will show prove of sources of income before he can open a letter of credit. Import and export monopoly will not be allowed, a case where certain powerful elements in the nation are granted permission to import essential commodities while other importers are denied the same right should end.Again,to combat bribery and corruption at our seaport and airport the government have to find a different ways to collect customs import revenues,[1] one method is to make sure that importers and clearing does not have directly contact with customs and customs examiners and port workers while on official business, [2] importers and the clearing agents can only stop at the custom's long room where they will submit their shipping documents and wait until after goods are examined and approved then they pick up their documents in order to remove their cargo from the port, [3] customs duties and ports charges should be combined in one application form so that importers can make one rump payment. The importers and clearing agents will not be allowed to go near cargo areas so woudn't have chance to bribe officials. Please dismantle all customs road blocks amounted in every nook and corners of the nation's high ways and streets.

The Nigerian Armed Forces

It appears that for more than forty years, the country's armed forces, which was once the pride of the nation, have been left untrained and underfunded. It is about time that the nation's military forces be returned as active, sharp, agile, and professional as they were known before the start of the civil war. It is time to return the Nigerian Armed Forces to the time in the past when they were trained and armed and were very active as well as admired, respected, and was the proudest thing for the nation.

The Nigerian people will be more than proud to see their armed forces returned back to its past glory. Nigerians will once again like to see a well-funded, trained, and disciplined armed forces of men and women equipped with the most sophisticated weaponry money can buy in the market for them to be able to defend the nation in time of an attack or war.

The recent Boko Haram menace in the country has really exposed how the nation's military has been left unprepared to defend the nation. The Nigerian Armed Forces and the nation's educational system should be placed as top priority in the nation's budget allocations.

The armed forces of Nigeria was underfunded by their former military generals, who became heads of state through military coups and later became civilian heads of state and were responsible for underfunding the Nigerian Armed Forces because according to some of them, they feared that the youths are joining the military for the sole purpose of overthrowing the government.

Here is an interview given by one of the nation's former military general and former head of state, General Obasanjo. General Olusegun Obasanjo explains his plan to curb the military according to him.

> The incursion of the military into government has been a disaster for our country and for the military over the last thirty years. Professionalism has been lost. Youths go into the military not to pursue a noble career but with the sole intention of taking part in military coups and to be appointed as military administrators of states and chairman of tasks forces. A great deal of orientation has to be undertaken and a redefinition of roles, retraining and reeducation will have to be done to ensure that the military submits to civil authority and regain its pride, professionalism and tradition. We shall restore military cooperation and exchanges with our traditional friends. (Obasanjo interview with McDougal of World History, New York Edition)

Well said and well-spoken, General Obasanjo. No one will doubt or second-guess your statement. However, there still remains many questions for Obasanjo to answer for the roles he played on about what he said about the military and country he led for twelve years to economic, political, and social ruin. If he indeed believed that military service is a noble profession and wanted to maintain it, then why did he immobilize it when he overthrew a legitimate government with his gangs in 1975? It is a good thing now that he has admitted that the military was wrong in the first place to overthrow legitimate governments.

Also, he has to admit that his twelve years of leadership of the country was a disaster that resulted to a failed state. He also should muster the courage to admit that he ruined the nation's economy with his decrees and public polices he initiated. He turned one of the most forward-looking, progressive African economies to ruin and disaster and created massive failures and poverty everywhere in the nation. He squandered and pissed off Nigerian oil wealth by taking care of himself, families, and friends while the masses suffered.

How can Obasanjo defend himself before the youths he is now accusing of joining the military for the sole purpose of overthrowing a government in order to become administrators when he himself staged a coup that overthrew a legitimate Nigerian government in 1975? Sir, General, Former President Olusegun Obasanjo, the youths are not joining the military because they want to be administrators or governors but because you destroyed their futures with your poisonous economic and social decrees for the twelve years you led the country.

President Obasanjo, the youths are not joining the military because they want to be administrators or governors but because their no job opportunity for them in which you are responsible because were their former leader.

Sir, you own the youths an apology for your false accusations against them. Let me remind you, joining the military for these youths you are now crucifying was a last resort for them because they had no choice. Due to your economic decrees, these kids cannot find jobs because your decrees killed the job market for them. Sir, put yourself in the shoes of these youths. If you found yourself in a similar situation of staying jobless for years, what could you have done? Sir, would you have folded your hands and done nothing. After graduating high school and university, can you live without a job? If no, what could you have done to have a job?

You joined the military with high school diploma and rose to become a military general, military head of state, and a president—not an easy achievement. Why did you not allow others to climb the same ladder you did by creating jobs when you led the country for twelve years?

Many university graduates have never found decent jobs for more than twenty years after graduation. Many of them gave up searching for jobs, and many turned to teaching, which pays less than fifty dollars a month. Your leadership wasted the future of generations of Nigerians. Sir, can you point to the youths just one single legacy you left behind that they and the country can remember you for? Some of them who can no longer endure hardships in their country engage in criminal activities, and many of them flee the country in droves to escape poverty on a daily basis, and the nation is losing its potentials to other nations. It is good that you have admitted the military was one time a noble profession. But who made it less noble? It was you who started the downfall of the military the very day you overthrew a legitimate government of Nigeria. After that act, your junior military officers followed your footsteps and overthrew governments in order to become presidents and administrators through the use of force, which you now admit that it was a complete disaster for the nation and the people. Your administration created lower and underclass citizens, the type that has never been seen in this country. Your decrees snuffed out a flourishing middle class in the nation forever. Who are you going to call a middle-class family in Nigeria today? If a graduate is lucky to find a job, he or she will receive a salary of between fifty dollars to two hundred dollars a month.

The hour has come to restore the Nigerian military to its former glory or better. The military must be trained to be involved in some high-tech civilian duties in peacetime. If possible, the government should be prepared to build a fortresslike military research center to attract military, civilian, and international scientists to come together in the country to research for both military hardwares and civilian hardwares.

Indeed, the hour has come that the government may choose to have the American and the NATO military bases at the country's backyard. This proposal should be taken seriously and be considered. For a nation to grow and succeed politically, economically, and socially, they must choose sides by seeking trusted allies to work with. The goal is to create the greatest happiness for the greatest number of people. The government should embrace the seriousness of changing from the old order to a new order and a new nation. A developing nation like Nigeria should not be afraid to ally itself to some powerful nations to protect and help them to advance into technology and bring jobs, electricity, water, roads, and so on and so forth.

President Jonathan Goodluck

In the 2011 presidential elections, he was seen as the lesser evil among the pack of presidential wannabes but with doubts on his ability to comprehend the problems facing the country because he has already served two years as vice president and two as president without any tangible achievements to his credit.

As always, Nigerians don't always have a choice when it comes to electing a president or other leader because at the end of the day, it will be decided on the basis of tribalism instead of a candidate's competence and agendas. Votes are sentimentally cast, therefore denying the people the chance to elect someone who is competent and knowledgeable about the problems facing the nation.

An avid political observer would have noticed that President Goodluck created his own nemesis that made him look like he was incompetent, and that was when he made his ministerial appointments. He became trolled the very moment that he announced rehiring the former finance minister from the World Bank as his new finance minister. No one would know or understand the reasons behind her rehiring because she has been around the corridor of power since 1999, when Obasanjo first hired her to be his finance minister and later as external affairs minister.

Since all these times she was made the nation's economic watchdog, the economy labored under hyperinflation, falling exchange rate, and an endemic unemployment situation continues. Anyone who was hoping that she will change her method of dealing with the nation's truckloads of economic problems was disappointed.

She refuses to pronounce the words *reforms, reforms,* and *end of the status quo* to the ears of her boss and Nigerians. She supported trade embargoes making Nigerians live on items lifted from European Dumpsters and smuggled into the country. The economy continues to lose billions and billions of dollars in smuggling activities because of trade embargoes. Every news coming out of the government on the status and performance of the economy were all full of lies because nothing actually changed but instead remains static.

Her Claims That the Economy Created 1.3 Million in 2013

Her claim that the economy created 1.3 million jobs in 2013 was false and the biggest insult to millions of unemployed Nigerians. There was no statistics to prove this claim. She didn't tell Nigerians in what sector of economy these jobs were created.

Let us assume that this claim can be believed. Then the question should be, Why for more than thirty-eight years, high school graduates in the country have never found jobs or have never worked in their lives? Why is that university graduates wait for years or sometimes forever to find a job? Why is it that almost every youth, housewives, men, women, and university graduates have joined the army of petty trading to survive instead of getting jobs after their education? How can she claim that the economy created 1.3 million jobs in a nation that can only boast of 2,001 companies? How can she claim that the economy created 1.3 million jobs in a nation where there is no electricity, no running water, no roads? How can she claim that the economy created 1.3 million jobs in a nation where the youths are fleeing the country in droves to escape unemployment?

President Johnathan and his finance minister cooked the book because nobody in the country ask them question. There is no reliable scientific data to confirm whether the economy as claimed created 1.3 million jobs in 2013. It was all lies?

Another biggest unconfirmed claim was that the Nigerian economy GDP is more than 700 billion to one trillion dollars. The Johnathan administration claim that the economy is worth one trillions of dollars may be true but how will they prove it in a country that is suffering from high unemployment rate and over eighty percent of the citizens are petty traders. It is so sad to say the least that with all the oil wealth this country can only boost of two thousand and one [2001] companies throughout the country for a population of more than one hundred and eight million people. It is far way impossible to compare this with New York City which can boost of more than one million companies for a population of just eight million people. Why is that about 94 percent of the states do not have a single company? Why is that local governments have zero companies? With the GDP so high as stated, why are Nigerians still existing on one dollar per day? Why is that some graduates who are lucky to get a job are paid between one hundred to five hundred US dollars a month, which will never make ends meet because of hyperinflation? Why is it that there is no electricity, no clean water, no roads, no health care, no hospitals, no quality education, no jobs, no welfare for the poor? These are few parts of the crisis facing the nation today that is waiting for the "Superman" and reforms.

EDUCATION

Jonathan's second major failure was education. I thought, as he was a former university professor, that education will be his petty project. My belief was that he will make sure that the entire educational system will go through comprehensive reforms, but that never happened. It was so sad. I guess that every Nigerian who cared about education was disappointed, especially when he stayed and watched as university students were sent home and schools were shut down for almost one year and he did nothing. That incident offered him the greatest opportunity to reform the nation's educational system, but he failed to seize that opportunity to do something to end the recurring school closures every year. Nothing has changed in the nation's educational system because he left it unattended and allowed the status quo to continue.

His only success was awarding more pay to the university teachers and nothing for the students and their parents. Today, the nation's educational system that is supposed to be the gateway of training the nation's future leaders is in disarray and still waiting for the "Superman" to come. I urge that independent spies should be sent into these educational institutions to spy on its daily activities. Nigerians will raise alarms when they learn the outcome of the investigation is reported about what is going on inside the nation's so-called ivory tower. This same thing is happening inside the universities' teaching hospitals. I am very sorry to say that the nation's institutions are rotten and waiting for reforms.

When poor parents manage to pay their children's school fees, the professors will demand for professor fees, instructor fees, office fees, clerk fees, blackboard fees, test handout fees, and chalk fees that have absolutely nothing to do with the school's official fees charged to students. Though the school administrators are fully aware about these illegal fees professors and staff collect from these poor students, they do nothing. In fact, if you step inside these institutions, you will instantly feel sorry and sympathize with these poor children on what they go through daily to obtain an education. Once again, the nation's president did nothing but instead abandoned them even though he was a university professor before becoming president. The president walked away.

Boko Haram

His initial handling of the kidnapping of over two hundred schoolchildren was a national disgrace. This incident was his third major mistake as a president. By the time he moved from vice president to president, Boko Haram was becoming a menace to the nation, but he paid only a lip service to it until it turned sour.

On one fateful day on Christmas morning in 2010, when families and friends gathered in a church in Abuja, the seat of power to worship and celebrate Christmas, hundreds of worshippers were slaughtered with bombs planted in the church by Boko Haram. Many others were injured. Many children were left orphaned. Wives were left widows, husbands were left widowers, and the government never cared. This single act alone would have spurred the president to take on Boko Haram head-on, but that never happened. Boko Haram increased and perfected their terrorist activities while the authority sat idly and watched. From 2010 to 2014, after the Abuja bombings, many such incidents have occurred, claiming tens and thousands of Nigerian lives. These innocent souls were slaughtered by Boko Haram either in the church, markets, schools, streets, or just simply right outside their houses. Still, the government did nothing. Thousands of children became fatherless, and wives and husband became widows and widowers. The government never cared to compensate them nor even had the courage to give scholarships to these affected children for them to continue their education. Instead, they were left to suffer and fetch for themselves.

The climax came in 2014 when about 219 young schoolgirls were kidnapped by Boko Haram terrorists at Chibok in North East

Nigeria. For a good three weeks the government of President Jonathan attempted to keep the information under the carpet, and they nearly succeeded, as usual. But thanks to the international community, the almost hidden act was exposed to the world and to Nigerians. Despite the exposure, the government continued to drag its foot and pretended as if it never happened until world leaders and first ladies, among them was Michelle Obama, joined forces to denounce it and demanded for the return of these girls. That is when the Nigerian government began to do something even though whatever action they took was still lukewarm.

The question is, Where was the president, the minister for education, the police chief, and Nigerian secret service officials for the first twenty-four hours after the kidnappings? Who was truly in charge of the nation? What defense does the government have to give for trying to hide this deadly act against innocent young schoolgirls?

From the onset of Boko Haram menacing the nation, the executive branch and legislative branch did not try to set up inquiries to investigate the activities of Boko Haram and their sources of funding, training, and their source of arms acquisition before it got out of control.

Who made the chief of army staff the presidential spokesman to repeatedly lie to Nigerians and the world that the girls have been seen and that they are coming home? He repeated it over and over for days and months, and still today we have not seen the girls return home or know their whereabouts. Innocent children who want to get education get stolen and the government chooses to lie about it? The army chief of staff should have left politics to politicians. He should have kept quiet and talked only about the military aspect of the search-and-rescue efforts instead of becoming a pawn for the president.

I think the reason why the 219 school girls kidnapped from their school was never found was because the government wasted too much valuable time to respond to the tragedy of the 219 kidnapped school girls they were lost. It took the government three weeks to even acknowledge that the kidnapping happened.

If the president was serious about finding those girls, who among his top officials did he hold accountable for failure of duty? How many did he fire? The president failed to hold any of his services chiefs accountable or punish any of them for their failure to respond accordingly after the kidnapping of these girls.

Why did the legislative branch of the government fail to probe the kidnapping and its aftermath? Why did the senate and representatives not inquire to know why it took the president and members of his staff three weeks after the kidnapping to respond?

Fuel Shortages

Who will believe that in an oil-producing nation that the people are still experiencing recurring fuel shortages year after year? It is shameful, to say the least. The reasons are not far-fetched because the country's leaders dubiously sold oil wells and refineries to some unscrupulous Nigerian profiteers who were not qualified to buy these megaventures that required a lot of talents and finances to own and run. Many of these dubious Nigerians claimed to be the richest people in the world even though they cannot account for the sources of their wealth if asked to do so.

Ganging Up Against the President

The first time I heard these words, "Ganging up against the president," was in a statement made by a former governor of one of the states in Nigeria during his interview with a BBC news reporter.

He stated that some people in the nation were ganging up against President Jonathan.

He also stated that the president cannot jump into a car and chase after Boko Haram to rescue the 219 kidnapped girls. Well, Mr. Governor, the president could jump into a car and chase after Boko Haram in many different ways as the head of state. But why did it take the president three weeks to respond to this tragedy? He could have visited the scene of the kidnapping as a show of support and show of force that will send a clear message to Boko Haram that the president is in charge and ready to crush them. The purpose of his visit would have been to fraternize with the victims' families and assure them that their children will be found and returned to them. Where was the minister for education, the army chief of staff, and the inspector general police? Why did they not immediately visit the scene of the kidnapping to talk to victims' families and assess the situation. Were the victims' families compensated? Was this statement made about "ganging up against the president" another myth and rumors and tribalism as usual in the country because some other Nigerians made the same statement? But it is all about excuses for a failed government.

Election Period

During the presidential elections, rumor started flying around that the kidnapping of the 219 schoolgirls never happened, that it was a lie and a gang-up against the president, and can you believe that this false information stuck in the nation even though there is abundant evidence to prove that the girls were kidnapped. Would you call this rumor an ignorance of facts or just simple naïveté displayed by some of these citizens to favor Jonathan in the election? Was it a setup to help the president win reelection?

Although Jonathan may have been the president of the nation, the way the political system is structured has made it often impossible to govern. That is the reason why I am advocating for reforms, for the nation to go back to the drawing board and start all over again with the body and soul of a virgin.

Cassava and Its Support from the Finance Minister

For sure the finance minister has been around the corridor of power for almost sixteen years, and as a political appointee, that would be considered in a civilized country to be too long, and couple that with the fact that her boss has since retired.

One of the most important things people expected to hear from her was to tell her bosses that the nation was in dare need of reforms, reforms, reforms, reforms! It is hard to fathom how a nation in this condition can stabilize its economy without the empowerment of the private sector economy. A nation of more than 180 million people could only boast of 2,001 companies, most of them banks that really do not impact the economy.

Government has formed the habits of creating irrelevant after irrelevant ministries and agencies instead of supporting the private economy system. The government spends billions of dollars for overhead costs to keep these ministries functioning. The ministries' purposes can only be found on its name; other than that, they are useless to the public and a waste pipe. It is more of a house of fraud, bribery, and corruption than a place of work. If the government has chosen to reform the nation as a whole, it could benefit from new international investments. Almost everybody in the world knows the country as a corrupt nation, and without reforms, it would be difficult to attract businesses to come to the country. Nations that respect business ethics will be weary of investing in Nigeria because of institutionalized bribery and corruption. A nation like Nigeria, which has deliberately sanctioned itself from conducting business with the outside world, cannot expect to stabilize its economy. This policy has led to junk goods after junk goods lifted from European countries' Dumpsters to be smuggled into the country. Paying the Paris Club was good, but reforms should have occurred first.

The Stimulus Package

Nigerians would like President Jonathan and his finance minister to account and tell them and the world what happened to almost ten billions dollars they gave to the government's four big banks in the name of stimulus package. They should also tell the people why many Nigerians didn't know about it. Why were no new jobs or opportunities created and no new critical infrastructures started with the stimulus package? Tell the nation who and who were given loans and if it was paid back. Why give this money directly to the banks that never give credit and loans to businesses and individuals to grow the economy? There are plenty of questions to be asked and be answered regarding the whereabouts of the ten billion dollars belonging to the people.

They should also tell the public what happened to about one billion dollars of contract awarded to a Chinese businessman to construct a passenger's rail track from Abuja to Kano and Kaduna that never happened and was never heard of again. The contract was to last for one year, but it is now more than five years, and nobody has heard of it again. The next government should step in to investigate and probe these allegations to the satisfaction of the nation.

Cassavagates

The idea that cassava flour can replace wheat flour is good. But the question is, Why does the government get involved for something that should be left entirely to businessmen and businesswomen who are interested and want to invest in it? Why was the government directly offering loans to bread bakers who agree to convert their wheat bread baking machines to cassava baking machines? Why would the government offer to forgive 70 percent of the loans? Who and who are the cassava flour bakers that the government intended to offer loans to and forgive 70 percent of the loans?

The entire "cassavagate" thing is supposed to be the responsibility of the private sector economy and not the government, and that is the reason for objection and because this enterprise cannot create jobs or earn the government any revenue. It is also not exportable It was another dubious tactic often applied by rogue government to steal the people's money. And how is anyone sure that these loans will be repaid or used for its intended purposes or given to the right people. Emphasis should have been laid on export and rebranding it into other uses instead of on cassava bread because Nigerians will not buy cassava bread.

Although Nigeria is the world's largest producer of cassava by 99.1 percent a year, they do not export any of it; instead, it is used domestically as food. The reason I believe it is not exported is because it has not been organized as an international commercial product. Most people farm cassava for family use only. In addition to this, private businessmen and businesswomen have not shown interest to engage in the commercial production of cassava. Another barrier is whether the cassava produce in the nation met the international litmus test for cassava export since it is not every country is allowed to export cassava.

The government also has not considered it as another source of revenue since it depends on oil for everything. This has to change; the nation has to empower the private sector economy to invest in this cassava project as export goods. That is the only way the nation can reap the benefits of cassava both as a revenue earner and as a job-creating enterprise.

Take for example the following countries: Thailand is the largest exporter of dried cassava with 77 percent export. Vietnam exports about 13.6 percent of their cassava production. Indonesia exports about 5.8 percent of their cassava production. Costa Rica exports about 2.1 percent of their cassava production. India has the most productive cassava farms in the world with a nationwide average yield of 34.48 tonnes per hectare in 2010. China is also the largest export market for cassava products from Thailand and Vietnam for a total of about 7 million tonnes a year.

Cassava is also one of the richest fermentable substances for the production of alcohol.

Nigeria can no longer bet all their hope on oil alone. They should learn to diversify and expand their means of revenue earning power and enable them to create jobs for their citizens.

Government should lay more emphasis on organizing cassava farming by empowering the private sector economy and welcoming interested international investors with the technology, technical know-how, finances, and experience to farm and to create cassava production factories that are capable of paying living wages to Nigerians.

Examples of other ways the nation as a whole can benefit from cassava farming are as follows:

- Biofuel: Cassava as an ethanol biofuel feedstock. Cassava (topical) chips have become the major source for ethanol production. China has completed the largest cassava

- fuel production facility, which has an annual output of 200,000 tons, that will need an average of 1.5 million tons of cassava. A China-based Hainan group has invested $51.5 million in a new biofuel facility that is expected to produce 33 million of bioethanol from cassava plants.
- Animal feed: cassava tubers and hay are used worldwide as animal feed. (Wikipedia.com)

Instead of the government laying emphasis only on converting wheat baking machines to cassava bread making machines by promising to forgive 70 percent of the loan received, the government should emphasize on encouraging interested small business owners to consider commercial cassava farming outposts and cassava facilities where cassava production can be made to be more productive for the nation. To achieve these goals, the government should consider allowing interested foreign farmers to come in and invest in cassava farming by mapping out farming areas around the country. The government should not get involved in financing any of these projects; it should be 100 percent private sector economy responsibilities. After all, the so-called cassava bread federal loans can only be given to the 1 percent rich Nigerians, who will never use it for the intended purposes but bank it in their private bank accounts and claim to be billionaires without visible means of livelihood.

The Nigerian National Congress and States Assembly

Since the beginning of the second republic in the year 1999, a good political observer will notice that nothing has changed since the beginning of this august body.

First and foremost, it is shameful that at the national congress, their first order of business is to fight for who and who will be the senate president and the speaker of the house decided on the basis of tribalism and the federal government, who likes to intrude when such selections are being made to choose a leader.

Who Are the Members of the National and State Assemblies?

An assembly of lame duck and rubber-stamp men and women who cannot make laws and cannot challenge the president on some of his unproductive policies cannot represent anyone. An assembly that is only interested in their personal aggrandizement and personal development cannot make laws for the nation. An assembly member who only wants freebies cannot make laws. Assembly members who hide away from their constituents cannot make laws. Assemblymen and assemblywomen who engage in bribery, fraud, embezzlement, and corruption cannot make laws. Assemblymen and women who abandon their constituents and take residence in luxurious rent-free, gated government homes with free cars, drivers, gas, maids, medical care, and food at the federal capital and state capitals cannot make laws for the nation. An assembly chamber that has never discussed, argued, probed any serious issue facing the nation since its inception cannot make laws for the nation. Assembly chambers that have never introduced, debated reforms are not fit to make laws for the nation. Assemblymen and assemblywomen who have never brought bacon home to his or her constituents are not fit to be elected as representatives of their people. An assembly chamber where its members failed to pass a bill to end trade embargoes put in place for more than forty years, which is suffocating the economy. An assembly chamber who refuses to pass rent control laws, that leaves the citizens at the mercy of the nation's Sherlock landlords and their attorneys, is not fit to represent anyone. An assembly chamber where the opposition is in concord with the president 100 percent of the time is not qualified to be an opposition. Do you think that many of these assembly members know their responsibilities to the nation and why they are elected?

With the freebies they get and heavy salaries and benefits they award to themselves and them failing to live up to expectations, it is very sad. They never pass bills that change the current economic situation in the nation or advance any good idea on how to create jobs for Nigerians. While the masses they claim to represent suffer, they swim in luxuries for doing nothing.

No president in this country has ever governed with any strong opposition; it is always "I agree," "I concur," and "Show me the money."

The hour has come when lawmakers will no longer be given free walled and gated compounds far away from the people they claim to represent. The hour has come that the days of free cars, fat salaries, free drivers, free gas, free maids, free health care, and free food should come to an end in this nation, where families and children go to bed with empty stomachs.

The hour has come when every assembly member will take residence in his or her community or districts that they represent at national and state levels and will not allow to live in free houses in the federal and state capitals because it is a big letdown and shame that these men and women abuse their power with impunity and assault the sensibility of the people of Nigerian as if they are fools.

Can you believe that the country's do nothing assembly members earn more moneythan the United States president and the members of US congress. Though the country still labors under the highest unemployment rate in the world yet these members of congress remain clueless about the daily struggles of those they represent who are finding it difficult to put food on the table for their families. Those Nigerians who have jobs are paid starting from, ten cent, twenty cent, twenty five cent and fifty cent an hour and they work twelve hours a day and seven days week without vacation. At the end of the month majority of them are not paid some of them are owned back pay for more than a year.

Real Estate Markets

The assembly members and the president pretend as if they are not aware of what is going on in the real estate market in the nation. For this reason, it is time for the assembly members to begin to rent their apartments when they travel to their jobsite; the government shall no longer be responsible in providing free accommodations to them.

They should go into the town to find an apartment to rent from the landlords and their attorneys, and let's see if they will pay the atrocious rent and fees demanded by the Nigerian Sherlock landlords. Because of the high unemployment rate and the suffering bunch of Nigerians are facing today the government should not continue to fund the free living styles of the members of congress both federal and states. Rent free luxurious house being given to them. Today, landlords and their attorneys demand two to three years rent in advance, landlord kola nut fees, landlord association fees, attorney's fees and agent fees from a poor man who is looking for place to live. This is some of the ugly experiences Nigerians go through to find and rent a place to live. No member of the state or national assembly should be given a free house. They should rent their own apartments. They should go and rent from the Nigerian Sherlock landlords, attorneys and housing agents demand extra free money after collecting two to three rents in advance. The extra money they collect from these helpless tenants is nicked, landlord kola nut fees, landlord's association fees, the attorney fees and agent's fee which is equal to one year rent stolen from these helpless Nigerians. It is time for somebody to end this practice because it is an injustice. I urge these men and women to sit up and pass a rent edit law to protect Nigerians from these Sherlock lords and their attorneys. They should pass a rent law that only allows the lords to charge one month rent, one month deposit and ten percent as agent and no attorney fees.

The president and the lawmakers are aware of the antics of these Sherlock landlords but did nothing. The government must take action to stop this punishment landlords and their attorneys inflict on their fellow citizens because they want to rent a place to live—rent demands that majority cannot afford. People are made to become criminals in order to find money to meet this atrocious demand from the landlords and their attorneys. It is very sad indeed. Is this the way our country will develop? If these men and women no longer want to be lawmakers or cannot make laws for the nation, they better find something else to do because the time has come that Nigerians no longer have the patience and will take action to recover their country from these sharks by whatever way necessary.

Rent Control

As the nation embarks on reforms, new rent control laws should be enacted to protect renters from the Sherlock landlords and their attorneys. Throughout the federation, no landlord will be permitted to demand for more one month's rent, one month's deposit, and 10 percent for housing agent. No attorney fees, no landlord fees, no landlord association fees should be demanded from a prospective tenant. All this is about effort to create some form of decent society where laws are obeyed.

Opposition Parties

The nation lacks coherent opposition party because all the parties are the same birds that flock together. Have you heard or seen a senator or a representative who fervently defended his principles or beliefs at the chambers floor or outside of it? Have you heard or seen any member introducing a bill that would help reform the nation and was successfully passed into law? Have you heard or seen any member calling community meetings with their constituents to inform them and tell them about government services at the national and state levels? Ask anyone of them what effort they have made to bring businesses in the community to help create jobs. Have you heard or seen them introducing free education from PK4 to high school? Have you heard or seen anyone introducing a bill to give schoolchildren from PK4 to high school free breakfast and lunch? Have you seen or heard them introducing a bill to light the nation, bring clean water, build roads, introduce technology, and end national certificate examination, which is only a fraud? Have you seen or heard anyone introducing bills to end bribery, embezzlements, fraud, and corruption? Have heard or seen any committee member investing and probing serious matters arising in the country? Have you seen or heard any one of them challenge or reject any unwanted president's public policy? Many of them don't even know what lawmaking means; they are just there to rip the people off and get rich overnight. Even if they made a mistake to have a case investigated or probed, no good thing will come out of it. Let them give an example of a serious matter about the nation they have handled and settled since they were elected years ago.

The Anambra-Delta States

It is either because of tribalism or because the two states wait for their monthly allocations they get from the federal government or just simple lack of vision that made them not realize their potentials. The two states have lots of potentials and resources to put together that will earn them higher revenues and help them to create thousands of jobs for Nigerians. But the states ignored these opportunities and failed to explore them for their benefits. The two states, I guess, are not aware that they are strategically positioned to be an economic powerhouse without the input of the federal government.

For example, the two states could form an organization such as Anambra-Delta Metropolitan Transport Authority (ADMTA) that will include the Anambra-Delta International Airport (ADIA), Anambra-Delta Ports Authority (ADPA), Anambra-Delta Ferry Services (ADFS), Anambra-Delta Land Transportation Services (ADLTS). In which, both families will be combined to be known as Anambra-Delta Metropolitan Transport Authority (ADMTA). In which, their joint ventures will include taking over the control of power supply and clean water by signing a contact with international investors to take charge in fixing and building these critical infrastructures for the states. Instead, they wait for the federal government handouts to run their government. The joint ventures could have helped the two states to earn a huge amount of joint revenue and create thousands, if not millions, of direct and indirect jobs for their citizens.

Anambra State Main Market Stock Exchange

Except the governor, no one else can tell the idea behind putting up beautiful mansions in the name of building a stock exchange market where majority of the people are petty traders and have no companies or stock exchange traders. Nobody can really tell what the former governor of Anambra State, Peter Obi, was thinking when he spent billions of naira to build what I called the Onitsha Traders Main Market Stock Exchange even though the state does not have a single functioning company nor does it have jobs for its citizens. Since after it was built, it has remained abandoned to rats and roaches.

The only better use for this abandoned building is to convert it to University of Onitsha or be named Major Chukwuma Kaduna Nzeagwu University. The institution will help to educate the main market traders who may become future stock traders. Beside Onitsha is the commercial nerve of the state and is more than qualified to have a university because of its strategic economic position to the state. Onitsha is overdue for a higher institution of learning because high school graduates who no longer can find a job are all traders at the main market. Many of them want to further their education, but there is no nearby university for them to attend, so the proper uses for these buildings is converting them into a university which will offer the opportunity to achieve their dreams and help the state.

The former governor Peter Obi of Anambra State initiated Computer Gate, which merits probe. The same state governor awarded billions of naira worth of contracts to contractors to purchase computers for schools. But the contractors ended up buying used equipment that was abandon. And the state lack electricity and computer teachers something that would have been put in place first.

Brief Words About Igbos

The Igbo people are a very fascinating and smart people. Before the civil war, they were well regarded, respected, admired, loved, and envied by many Nigerians because of their industriousness, hard work, intelligence, and creativeness.

I have never forgotten, and I still remember, being a boy from the sixties, the National Igbo Union Day celebrations, which usually was the biggest day of unity, peace, love, happiness, dancing, drinking, and eating throughout the country for Igbos and friends. It was a day set aside by the Igbos to come out in full force to showcase their culture, heritage, and talents throughout the federation. As powerful and joyful as this Igbo Day celebrations were, every Nigeria joyfully joined in to celebrate with the Igbos in high spirits.

The Igbos in those days were a strong, united group that was the envy of Nigerians. The Igbos had a very strong emotional attachment to their union and groups, which made them an indivisible and impenetrable and unbroken force. They could communicate to each other with only eye contact.

The center of attraction on the day of the Igbo Day celebrations was the Arbriba warrior dancers that everybody wanted to see dance. It is a powerful cultural war dance that only really macho men can handle. They step out and dance with the greatest majestic steps and styles and manner that you can't help but to love and be jealous of them. The Igbos were quite displeased and disappointed when the federal government outlawed the union before the Nigerian civil war began.

Without explanation, the federal government outlawed the Igbo union before the start of the civil war. After the civil war, the Igbos had never summoned up courage to jump-start and organize themselves into another formidable Igbo union but instead chose to walk like sheep without a shepherd. Today it is difficult to find an authentic Igbo leaders unlike before the civil war. The reasons are not farfetched most Igbos love to chase and buy titles instead of helping his brother or her sister to succeed. They separated themselves on the basis of dialectal royalty because of these they no longer can communicate effectively as a common group to support and help each other.

Igbo Politics

Before the civil war, the Igbo politicians were head and front in Nigerian politics. It could be right to say that Igbo politicians championed the fight for Nigerian independence. Some of the well-known Igbo luminaries who patriotically fought for the attainment of Nigerian Independence were as follows: Chief Mbaonu Ojike, Dr. Nnamdi Azikiwe, Dr. Mike Opkara, Dr. K. O. Mbadiwe, Chief R. B. K. Okafor, Dr. Akanu Ibam, Chief Dennis Osadebey, and so many others to mention. Sadly enough, Chief Mbaonu Ojke, the main architect of the fight for Nigerian independence, died before his dreams came true.

The federal government and the people of the former eastern region need to honor this wonderful, patriotic Nigerian, Chief Mbaonu Ojike, who died while fighting for independence. He should be properly honored.

The Igbo Presidency

Throughout the history of Nigeria, the Igbos have contributed immensely to the development of Nigeria, beginning from the first day of the fight for independence. But one thing has consistently eroded the Igbos in Nigeria, and that is attaining the presidency of the country

Though during the postindependence national election, Dr. Azikiwe and many other Igbo leaders were evidently more than qualified to be elected as the first prime minister of Nigeria, but that did not happen and has never happen for more than fifty years after the Igbos fought and won independence for Nigeria. This is an injustice.

After the War Ended

Since after the end of the civil war, the Igbos have ventured into Nigerian national politics, trying to reclaim their past political glory but have not been successful in doing so. These days the Igbos appear to be tired of Nigerian politics because of their low acceptance by other Nigerians. Igbos today seem to choose to wait for the crumbs that fall from the masters' table instead of being the masters themselves.

It was shameful enough to say that the Igbos have abandoned its political interest and responsibility of protecting its group's civil rights and by contributing to raise their voices about the injustices in the nation. They rather chose to pursue fly-by-night wealth all over the world instead of pursuing sustainable wealth in their country. This quest for quick gratification at all costs has alienated the Igbos away from Nigerian politics and social and economic power play.

The Igbos since after the civil war ended have never held or controlled any form of power or authority in Nigeria. They have been in a political limbo for too long. I believe that their forebears who fought and won independence for this country will be turning in their graves on what has become the Igbo man today in regard to their God-given rights in Nigeria. They have woefully, woefully disappointed these men and women who sacrificed their lives for their sake and the country. The Igbos must once again step out to demand and claim their right to be president of Nigeria. Igbos deserve it.

One Igbo Man, One British Twenty Pounds Sterling

After the civil war ended and the country welcomed the Igbos back to Nigeria as citizens, the federal government decreed that the Igbos would be given twenty British pounds sterling per man even though they had deposited billions of British pounds in banks all over the nation. The government refuses to return the money in full to the rightful owners.

The Igbos did not argue but accepted the offer because they had no choice, and they had lost all their possessions during the war. But the most surprising thing was that those of them who were lucky to be given the twenty British pounds sterling used it to start a petty trade and within a year turned it into megamillion-naira enterprises. They became millionaires by starting a petty trade with just twenty pounds. It was amazing, to say the least. Soon they moved from petty trading to starting big local and international businesses all over the country. Soon all these businesses would go under because of government trade decrees that snuffed out these successful businesses with a twinkle of an eye. And they came back in full force to save the nation's economy through smuggling goods and their ability to bribe government to access these contraband.

The Igbos As the Most Cosmopolitan Nigerians

There is no single Nigerian that will not attest or agree that the Igbos are the most cosmopolitan Nigerians who have emigrated to every nook and corner of the nation. They have developed villages into towns and cities all over the country. Any village or town they entered, they will open up businesses, build houses, introduce transportation, schools, and markets, and energize the communities to participate in every activity that will help them to grow economically. There is no other Nigerian that has emigrated and traveled around the country like the Igbos. If other Nigerians emigrated the way the Igbos does, tribalism, nepotism, and favoritism wouldn't engulf Nigeria.

Igbos developed many areas of business; among them are fashion, motor parts business, which made those who engage in it millionaires. Others were import and export, fashion, music. They traveled around the world importing goods and merchandise home, but remember, they started with only twenty British pounds.

But by 1976, when Obasanjo became the head of state and introduced his dictatorial economic decrees, which the Igbos as traders paid the greatest price for, their businesses were seriously affected, and many lost their businesses and their means of livelihood. Trust the Igbos; they never give up when it comes to making money

The Fallout of the Poison Economic Decrees in the 1990s

The Nigerian people must always be grateful to the Igbos for saving the country from total economic collapse. By the beginning of 1990s, the dictatorial economic decrees enacted by the military leaders in the seventies and eighties had come to hit the country like a tsunami. The nation's economic system was on life-support. The military economic decrees, such as indigenization, naturalization, second-tier market and the trade embargoes, have collapsed the economy, creating so much hardship for the people.

There was scarcity of everything from food, clothing, jobs, vehicles, motor parts, housing—name it. If you are lucky to have a job, there are chances that you will not be paid for up to a year or more. Pensioners were never paid again. Nigerians can no longer account for their visible means of livelihood. It was mayhem, a dog-eat-dog kind of life existence. Many took to crime to survive. Armed robbery increased. Interstate buses were ambushed at the dead of the night and robbed. After which, they killed so many of the passengers or outrightly set the passengers and the buses ablaze. The Nigerian police forces could not do anything; some of them aided and abetted the armed robbers.

Because the Igbos had lost their jobs and businesses, they jumped into action to save the Nigerian economy. Many of them fled the country and went to Europe and all over the world. In Germany they found and gathered cars, especially Mercedes cars, smuggled them into the country or through neighboring countries. They smuggled used motor parts, food, clothing, housewares, and so on. Most of these items were lifted from Dumpsters.

By the 2000s, because of the Igbos, Nigerians were once again able to buy used old-model Mercedes cars smuggled into the country from Germany, and soon it became a common sight. They smuggled used goods of all types into the country, and people were able to afford these items that only the rich in the nation could buy. Today used vehicles and used goods are smuggled into the country from all over the world. The people have no choice but to patronize these used goods. The trade embargoes and ban on importation initiated by the military leaders were penny-wise and pound-foolish economic decrees that nearly destroyed the country. It inflected the worst hardships on the people and the nation. This economic measure failed to achieve or change anything in the nation's economic system. The pain remains.

Though the Igbos saved Nigeria from imminent economic collapse, they neither hold political nor economic power or make decisions in the nation, yet they control and dominate the nation's commerce. Despite all these efforts, their contribution to regrow the economy after it collapsed was not understood by other Nigerians because they hated them for being smart. The Igbos are despised by many other Nigerians because of their hard work.

The North and Western Nigeria Politics: The Hausa and the Youraba

For almost fifty years now, the northern and western military officers, police officers, and politician have ruled Nigeria without the Igbos. They are responsible for whatever happened whether good or bad; they are the ones to give the nation an account of what good policy or bad policy was enacted, whether their leadership was successful or not successful for the past half a century that they have been ruling the country, whether their policies and decrees throughout their time in leadership resulted to Nigeria being referred to as a failed state. They are also in a better position to give an account to Nigerians about the missing oil wealth. They took advantage of the civil war to push the Igbos out from holding political and economic power.

Northern Nigeria's and Western Nigeria's Most Admired Political Icons

The most popular postindependence political icon from Northern Nigeria was Ahmed Bello, the Saduna of Sokoto and the former premier of Northern Nigeria, who was a very charismatic Nigerian leader. He impacted strong leadership styles throughout the nation. He was a beloved leader who was worshiped by his people. It was so sad that the first sign of Nigerian trolley problems claimed his life prematurely. He believed in Nigerians and fiercely defended his constituents against any foreign interference. He was highly admired by so many Nigerians because of his vision for the North and the whole nation. He was a very intelligent leader who contributed so much to the development of the nation. He was an irreplaceable political icon. As a kid, I admired him so much. His followers from Northern Nigeria are referred as Sadunaist movement, who you will find holding power in the military, police, customs, immigration, politics, and every top federal government office position. They rule the country, and they are the nation's decisions makers.

Chief Awolowo, the former premier of Western Nigerian turned opposition leader, was jailed for treason. When he was set free because of the echo of the civil war, he was appointed Nigerian finance minister at the start of the civil war. After the civil war ended, he initiated a plan to give the Igbos twenty British pounds each regardless of the billions of British pounds they had saved in Nigerian banks before the civil war, which they left behind when they fled to the eastern part of the country for their safety.

He also initiated the failed indigenization decree that destructed the Nigerian economy. Yet he was a very formidable opposition leader and was also a great leader of the Western Nigerian people.

He was the leader Nigerians never had. He also reneged on the promise he gave to General Ojukwu that if the East seceded, the West will also secede from Nigeria after General Ojukwu got him out of jail at Enugu prison yard, where he was jailed for treason. He has betrayed the Igbos in several occasions.

Chief Awolowo, no doubt, was a great leader of Western Nigeria, and his leadership style impacted the whole country in no small way. He was the strongest and toughest opposition leader, feared and respected and adored by his people. He always was ready for political combat with his rivals when it comes to defending his people. He was the best regional premier in terms of economic development of his region. He did a lot with the cocoa revenue. He introduced free education, built roads, and provided electricity and water in his region. He perhaps would have been a great national leader and president if he was given the chance. But he was also very tribalistic to the core. I also admired these two Nigerian iconic leaders. He was in the wrong when he seized billions of British pounds sterling the Igbos left in Nigerian banks before the war. He gave the Igbos twenty pounds sterling each, but only very few were lucky to get the money. His final act was decreeing indigenization of foreign businesses that snuffed the life out of the nation's economy.

Awolowo had his own followers from the West referred to as Awoist movement. You can also find them holding power as top military officers, top police officers, top customs and immigration officers, top political leaders, top federal government officials, and are also the nation's decision makers. With the bourgeoisies from the north, they have dominated the political, economic leadership of the nation for more than half a century now.

Although there is no law preventing the Igbos from being part of national leadership, their inability to brand into Nigerian politics in full may be attributed to the Nigeria-Biafra civil war because they lost everything they had and had to start all over again with little or nothing. When they returned from the war, there was no vacancy for them to participate in the decision-making body in the nation.

Dr. Nnamdi Azikiwe was one of the most sought-after Nigerian icons. He was all Nigerian without an atom of tribalism in him. He schooled in America and earned a PhD in politics. He was among the first groups of Nigerians who mounted the strongest fight for Nigerian freedom from the British colonial masters. Along with other Nigerians, they fought day and night until the nation was granted independence. Despite his sacrifice to the nation, he was rewarded with a ceremonial head of government position referred as the president general of Nigeria, instead of the prime minister. Very much like him, he graciously accepted it for the sake of peace and unity of the nation. His major political rival was Chief Awolowo. Dr. Azikiwe was a peaceful man who passionately loved his country and the people.

Throughout the civil war he was neutral because he believed in one Nigeria. He helped to end the war because he no longer was able to withstand the untold sufferings seen on the Biafra side of the war.

I believe he did the right to help to end the war. He was a statesman and a nice fellow. His followers are known as Zik's movement, but since the Igbos got fed up with Nigerian politics, I am not sure if they are still active. If not, the youth can reignite it for the sake of Nigerian politics.

The Igbos' Professions

Before the civil war the Igbo families invested heavily in the education of their children. They took it as a great pride to do so. Because of this, the Igbo youth did not join the military forces or police forces because at that time, higher educational certificates were not a requirement to join these forces The Igbos were becoming lawyers and medical doctors and were getting PhDs. Not until a political crisis began in Nigeria in the sixties did the Igbos realize that they made the mistake of not allowing their children to join any of the Nigerian armed forces. It was now clear that the Nigerian military forces will hold power for a foreseeable future.

Many Igbo families have produced medical doctors, PhD holders, lawyers, engineers, mathematicians, and so many others.

Because the Biafra side of the war lacked war equipment due to the economic brocade placed against them by the federal government of Nigerian, they were spurred into action. The Igbo scientists took the boldest action to build improvised weapons of war that were crudely made but yet turned out to be very effective and powerful to sustain the war and kept the federal army fighting for three years.

These scientists were able as well to crudely refine crude oil to produce fuel, gas, and kerosene to be used for the war and by the people.

These Biafra scientists crudely made the greatest weapon of the war nicknamed Mass Killer, which is known in the Western world as the atomic bomb.

The Igbos are geniuses that have gone unacknowledged by the federal government of Nigeria. After the civil war, the government due to tribalism, allowed these Biafra scientists to be wasted without finding how they made those powerful weapons of war with nothing. Many of them have died; if any one of them is living, he will be too old. These men could have been used to train future Nigerian scientists and could have helped to lead the nation into technological discovery. Instead, the nation's political power holders ignored the benefits of these valuable Nigerians.

The Igbo Presidency

The time has come to level the political playing field for every Nigerian no matter his or her tribe. We are all Nigerians and no one should be discriminated against.

Almost every other ethnic groups in Nigeria has been president except the Igbos. The Igbos are eminently qualified to be the president of Nigeria.

The Igbos who applied the twenty British pounds sterling the federal government gave some of them after the war to start petty trading and within a short period of time turned it into a megamillion dollars business enterprises is fit to rule Nigeria. The Igbos who hold no political or economic power but dominates the nation's commerce and are largely responsible in saving the country from immediate economic collapse after the poison military economy decrees brought down its economy to its face, are fit to be president of Nigeria.

When the poison economic decrees enacted by Nigerian leaders collapsed the economy it was the Igbos who sprang into action to breathe life back into the economy. Without the Igbos no one would have known where Nigerian could have been today. The economic fallout from the military economic decrees in the seventies and eighties hurts the nation and the people badly and it was the Igbos that rescued the nation today through smuggling of goods into the country. The Igbos were the ones mostly affected by the military economic decrees of the seventies and eighties because they are traders and businessmen and women. They lost their businesses and jobs because of trade embargoes placed on the nation, yet they turn around to save the nation.

The Next President

The next president of Nigeria should be the Igbos. It is not about the issue of tribalism or quota but because it is about time and they merit it and as well as being highly qualified! The Igbo forebears fought and won independence for the nation, and it is their time to experience what it means to rule their country

I had an opportunity to be in a group of Nigerians who said during discussion that the Igbos can never be the president of Nigeria? Let see if this statement is true or false, whether it is a federal government decrees or law made against the Igbos during and after the war.

The Igbos National Organization

The Igbos or indeed all the people of the former eastern region and other interested Nigerians can join together to form an interest group. The purpose of forming an interest group is to fight against injustice, social inequality, to protect their civil rights and that of everyone else in the society. Celebrate its heritage and culture. To promote solidarity, stability, and order, to promote love, unity and peace for all, to contribute to the nation building. Promote creation of jobs and opportunities for all and to maintain law and order, to keep the country one nation.

It is important for the Igbos to start another national organization with other interested Nigerians and everyone else to come together as members of the new union because your ideas and voices in matters affecting local and national interest is needed. To contribute to the economic, political and social development of the nation.

The hour has come when the Igbos and their friends will reinstitute the Igbos national organization; however, this time around it should go international as well. The Igbos national day of culture and heritage pride celebrations will enable them thank the nation, and thank their god for their blessings and failures. And to remember those men and women who fought for their freedom and to promise that they will continue to fight for the freedom of everyone. When a date is chosen for the day of national celebrations, it should involve the ones living abroad from America to Europe to China and so on and so forth. The celebrations should commece the same day, time, and hour all over the world.

The memory of the Biafra unknown soldiers who fought asnd died to defend the rights of the Igbos and others should always be remembered. A burial ground should be entombed in their honor to be celebrated at a particular date and day every year.

Nigeria/Biafra Issues

I passionately love Nigeria, and I believe many Nigerians do as well. I believe in one Nigeria, and I believe in diversity. However, there are so many Nigerians who are very bitter and agitated about the raw deals they have gotten in their country, such as, a one sided ruling of the nation by the same class of people for more than half century the bad economic, bad leadership, unemployment, lack of amenities and lack of opportunities. Despite all these complaints Nigerian should remain one and allow everyone to contribute to the nation's development

Thinking of recreating Biafra is not the Igbos' best solution to their current situation in Nigeria, but rather being one Nigeria will serve everyone better. The situation will definitely change in Nigeria no matter what, and the Igbos will once again be proud to be Nigerians. Every Nigerian is needed to make Nigeria a great nation!

The civil war had being fought and has ended on the basis of no winner, no vanquished. There should be no more war. Let everyone embrace peace, unity, and progress.

The Three Major Tribes

The Hausas, the Igbos, and the Yorubas are the majority groups, and before the civil war, they were the major political office holders. But after the civil war the Igbos have yet to claim their position as major political players and high office holders on the national level.

The Nigerian Immigration and Other Uniformed Officers at the Airport and Seaports

The evil act committed against tourist and business people coming to Nigeria by immigration officials and customs at nation's the airport and seaports

The federal government should dig into the activities and behaviors of the Nigeria immigration and customs officials at the nation's airports and seaports towards foreign businessmen and tourists. The report stated that these visitors asked to pay fortune to these officials in order to gain entry the country even though they have visas. They have been complaints from Chinese and people from other nations who were charged about 750 dollars for visa in some Nigerian embassy abroad, and when they enter the country another round of bribe of between 2,500 to 3,000 US dollars is again demanded by the officials to allow them entry.

One of the victims told me that even after she paid the money, she and her children were again stopped at the exist gate and arrested and accused of illegal entry. Acting on this accusation the officials again demanded 2 million naira, equivalent to 10,000 US dollars. She called her friend in China who knew some of the officials and helped to reduce the amount demanded to 1.5 million naira, which she paid, and she and her family were allowed to enter the country. This is a very big embarrassment to the nation.

The government must set up a board of inquiries to investigate this mater both at home and aboard and hold someone accountable. This is a disgrace to the nation and it is taking place at the gateway to the nation. It is unacceptable.

The immigration and passenger's bill of rights for arriving and departing passengers should be written and be always handed over to passengers whenever they use this service to know their rights. This nation will not expect to develop if it cannot fix the nation's problems.

The Housing and the Land Robbery of Festac Town

The federal government built a megatown in 1974–1976 initiated by General Gowon to hold all African festival in 1975 called Festac. However, General Gowon was overthrown before his dreams and ideas came true.

General Obasanjo, who overthrew him, took over the leadership. It was built as a modern housing estate with all the modern amenities you can think of. At the end of the festival, the government balloted the entire housing estates to some lucky Nigerians because during that period of time they still exist some honest citizens. Also the government reserved thousands and thousands of acres of land around the housing estates for future development of housing for Nigeria.

You can't believe it beginning from the eighties when the economic situation became so bad and unbearable that many of those who won the houses and apartments had lost their jobs, retired and those of them on pension were no longer paid because there was no money to pay them.

That is when bribery and corruptions engulf the housing estates. Based on the economic situation the federal government estates administrators seized on the opportunity to sale children play grounds, recreation houses, public parks, vehicles parks, any empty land seen in view were sold to corrupt Nigerians from, top military officers, top police officers, top government officials, drug pushers, 419ners, customs officers, immigration officers and traders who turned around to build mansions and shopping plazas on the federal government stolen properties they bought with ill-gotten wealth from the masses. They deprived the children and adults the use of well-constructed beautiful playgrounds and parks.

Not done yet, this same group of men and women approached the poor house and apartments owners and convinced them to sale their houses and apartments to them for peanuts because these families were hungry and need money to feed their families. So families sold government properties to these crooks. Once the most beautiful place to live in Nigeria has become an eyesore. You will be kind enough to call it a junk yard because junk yard itself will be shame because it look better! Illegal structures after illegal structures have been built in every nook and corners of the estates that reduce to a junk enclave. Remember properties been sold are government properties that were sold without permission from the government because the official entrusted to manage the estates got deeply involved in bribery and corruptions. They aided and abated the illegal sales of government properties by individuals.

Again you would think these crooks are done, but a wait minute they taking the advantage that Nigeria is a lawless nation. They connive with the management official of the Festac Town to sale undeveloped lands the government reserved for future housing development for Nigerian. Within a twinkle of an eye, thousands and thousands of acres of land reserved for the second phase of Festac Town future housing development had been sold to corrupt individuals with forged documents. The buyers were the same high ranking law enforcement official, high ranking government official, traders, customs officers, immigration officers, drug pushers, 419ners. Federal government properties have been stolen in a broad daylight without anyone raising an eyebrow. Breaking the law is second nature to over 80 percent of Nigerians.

Today the second phase of the Festac reserved for public housing has been stolen and converted to build private mansion and shopping plazas and storefronts despite the beautiful mansions the complex is still looking like a junk yard.

The irony of the whole situation is that the problem is widespread throughout the country. From Festac to every part of the nation where government have built housing for the people. Those who were lucky to get these houses or apartments will turn government property into their personal real estates. As soon as they are approached by crooks with blood money to sale government houses or apartments to them for millions of naira that the sellers cannot resist because they have never seen such money before

Abuja, the nation sit of power have taken the first position as the most corrupt and fraud nerve center for turning federal government public lands and public housing into individual mortgages.

Nigerian crooks go about with their bloody bags of money from office to offices and from housing complex to housings complex to connive with government official and government house owners to sale government property to them. This illegal sale of government property to few Nigerians with money is helping to artificially jack up real-estate value in the nation creating scarcity of housing and sufferings.

Solutions and Penalties

Except the government is not interested in fixing the nation and want to continue to function as a lawless nation, then what does it mean to have a country. First the government should set up a board of inquiries to investigate and probe these allegations to hold those responsible accountable. The government must lead with example of obeying the law. And to show that those who break the law must pay the society back.

For the Festac Town, Lagos, there are several options open for the government to take:

1. For those who knew too well that they buying children playgrounds, parks, and others and used it to build mansions and shopping plazas must return the property and

pay to those who illegally bought government lands must pay to reverse them back to what it was being used for before it was stolen. They must also face pay heavy penalty for their crimes. These entire properties should be recover, undo and revoked.
2. Those who illegally purchased houses and apartments from government tenants must forfeit it and return the properties back to the government. They also will pay heavy penalty for their crimes or even face jail term if charge for crime and try.
3. Those who are renting their houses and apartments out without government permission may forfeit their houses and apartments back to the government. They too may forfeit all the rents they have collected on the property and also pay a penalty for converting government property.
4. Every illegal building, structures, stores, churches, schools that was developed by private individuals which was not included in the original plans of the Festac Town must be demolish and the culprits pay heavy amount of money or may face jail if tried. How can individuals enter public housing complex to buy play grounds, parks and any empty space illegally purchase them and build mansions, apartment, buy government houses and apartments, build churches, schools and rent them out can't be explained.
5. Festac Town second phase lands sale was the mother of all lands crimes committed against the government and the people and must be revoked and, undo and return to the government no matter what it has been use for. Lands were sold and bought with forged documents that look like a clean paper. This land that the government reserved to build affordable housing for Nigerians has been hijacked by some few elements in the society to build private houses

and apartment. And turn around to become government landlords instead of the government being their landlords. The sale of government lands must be investigated, probe and those responsible will face jail punishment and fine. Nigerians must be reminded that bribery, corruption and fraud is a crime that does not pay and may come back to hurt anyone that engages on them.

The final options for government is to use its domain power to recover phase 1 and phase 2 housing projects. The entire housing development is now an eyesore and a junk yard. First, the government will also reserve the option to demolish the entire estates from phase 1 and phase 2 so it can be rebuilt better for Nigerian and making rent laws. So that this type thing will never happen again.

Land and Housing Fraud

Like Festac Town in Lagos, government lands and housing faces similar fate across the nation. Whether it is a federal government or states land and housing or apartments individual recipients has converted them to their personal mortgages aided by crooks who dangle millions of blood money on their faces to sale government houses and lands to them.

The government must determine whether it is interested in fighting corruptions, bribery and fraud in the nation. If do they effort should be made to search and recover all the stolen properties, revoked the sales. Those who sold and those who bought these properties should equally face the law. The illegal transactions of selling government lands and housing were carried out throughout the country which affected the federal government and states properties.

It is about time the government fight bribery, corruptions and fraud because it is hampering its effort for developments.

The Federal Capital, Abuja

Since its inception, the federal capital territory has become the center for lands and housing fraud that the government need to seriously look into because no nation can achieve any meaningful development if it is engulf in corruption, bribery and fraud as means of achieving ones goals.

The city of Abuja lands and housing was hijacked by few rich people, majority of them are top government officials and their friends and used them to build luxurious houses, apartments and shopping plazas that were price out of the reach of the common man. These luxurious development do not bring much of revenue to the government or create jobs for the people.

The government should take action to reexamine the lands sales in the capital city to find out the way and the manner it was acquired, who and who owns them, how much revenue does these properties contribute to the government purse and what type of jobs they create. They will also find out why these luxuries development by rich individuals took over the city, instead of building critical infrastructures needed to create jobs and opportunities.

As the government enter the seasons of reforms the government reserve the right to use domain power to move about 80 percent of these luxurious houses and shopping plazas out of the city to other part of the city after investigations to determine if the properties were legitimately acquired in order for them to retain their properties. After reforms these properties are needed to develop critical infrastructures instead of building luxuries for few elements. The government needs tax revenues to develop the nation

The entire city of Abuja capital needs a complete makes over to pave way for meaningful economic development. Reforms will spur international investors, including Fortune 500 companies who will need lots of spaces to establish their businesses and it will not be advice able for the government to leave them in hands of the sharks and crooks Abuja landlords. The government relocated these luxurious properties built on the lands stolen from the people

City Housing in New York

Could you imagining some rich American going to New York City housing offices to connive with official to sale play grounds, parks and other open spaces located inside the projects to them so they become the owners' lands and can build mansions and shopping centers and rent them out. They live free rent and no property taxes. Or can a New York City housing resident's sale their apartments to a private individuals that have nothing to do with city housing. That is exactly what happened in public houses in Nigeria.

The Evil of Oil Bunkering

Over 50 percent of the oil production is stolen through bunkering. Bunkering is not a small business that a poor man can engage into. According to PBS documentary the penetrators are top government official who occupied high government offices at Abuja and Lagos. They along with their cronies invested billions of US dollars to purchase bunkering ships to carry out their evil desire of depriving Nigerians of their oil money. The government may claim that they making effort to stop this evil but how can government prove its claim when it is the same government officials that are penetrating the evil? Can a thief catch a thief? The government must fan out these officials and set an example with them if they are charge for crime and found guilty they should go to jail. The government must also seek for a way to close the. lop holes that facilitates this evil act committed against the nation.

This big time oil bunkering lords are the nation's billionaires.

The Last Resort

I made a promise that towards the end of the paper I will reveal the meaning of the last resort that Nigerians may take if reforms fail.

Reforms must start from the top to down, but in case everything failed because the government cannot reform the nation and the masses continue to suffer. Nigerians will give the government more time to try to reform. But if it failed, then towards the summer of 2017, and the economy did not show a sign of life by the time the government would have laid the foundation for creating jobs and opportunities for the masses and didn't happen. Then the masses reserved the right to confront the government and decide the best cause of action to be taken to save their country.

Revolution

I promised that towards the end of this paper, I will reveal the answer to the last resort to be taken to fix Nigeria.

The masses if they want can choose the Martin Luther King Jr. type of nonviolent revolution to remove the government. But before this will take place Nigerian people will have to tell the current government in power to dissolved the government starting from the executive branch, the national assembly, state governor, state assembly, local governments. Every past and current politician must be banned from participating in politics for life. Also ban will also extend to top career government officials and top career diplomats the government will appoint care committee to take charge of the government for at least for not more than one year pending when reforms is completed and a new government is formed. Only caretakers will be appointed to take over the functioning of the government. No president nor governors will be appointed; if the government fails to achieve any meaningful reforms, the current government should be dissolved. The nation cannot continue to put a round peg in a round hole because it will always give the same result over and over again

If every other thing failed, then revolution will be the last resort to hand over the country to the masses. The day of the revolution will be chosen, and it will be named the Broom Day. Nigerians will purchase brooms in advance to be used for sweeping away the past and current politicians out of power and out of sight. All concerned Nigerians and our international friends will prepare for the Broom Day in advance, waiting when the official date of action is chosen. Foods and essentials will be purchased in advance that would last for at least one month because Nigerians will sit outside their houses with their brooms in hand, sweeping away the government until they leave and new government will be formed. Nobody will go to work or market, no school nor transport all over the country. If they don't leave at a certain time, then we will troop outside on the street to confront them because Nigerians will not give up because enough is enough. The sufferings must end.

Broom day will be a day chosen for national and international protest against the past and present leaders, politicians and political appointees among others to be swept out of power. Nigerians will be ask to buy their brooms in advance and keep them until a date is set. On broom day they will be no work, no school will open, no market and no transportation everybody will sit outside their houses and begin to sweep them away until all of them are gone. There is no time limit to end the protest until the objective is achieve. We invite our international friends and allies to join us to drive out these vampires who have misruled this country for more than half century. It is time for change. It is time to uproot, destroy, rebuild, bigger, better and stronger. We shall sit by the curb of our houses and apartments and begin to sweep them away until they are gone forever. Your god says, "Uproot, destroy, rebuild, and rebuild better, bigger, and stronger. Fear thou not for I am your God. I am with you. I have given you the power of victory and not the power of fear." Nigerians, God will fix your country if you do the right thing and hear his voice.

Conclusion

For a little over one year, I have been writing this paper due to the fact that I am a novice in the field of writing. But to my greatest surprise, I found out that writing is quite interesting and enjoyable, especially when it has a purpose and a message.

In the paper I have revealed the genesis of the nation's trolley problems and how it became a failed state in Nigeria in particular and African nations in general. Despite all these failures, I believe that the best is yet to come for Nigeria and Africa. I am very optimistic about Nigerian future because they have the potentials and resources to be a great nation. Mark this: without reforms, this nation is not going to change.

The underlining issue is whether Nigeria can successfully carry out reforms, but if it does, it will spur the Nigerians into actions. Government should place reforms as a top priority for the nation. Other issues for the nation are leadership problems that must be addressed during reforms. A nation where law and order are not obeyed has a big problem. The nation also has serious leadership problems when the majority of people who enter politics or join the government workforce do so for their personal pocketbooks.

There is no doubt that my encounter with a total stranger on the night of Dec.30, 2013 was a game changer that spur me to begin this book after I heard his story about the sufferings of the masses who are living in the midst of oil wealth. "Nigerians are tired and need help" I say it once again, Nigerians the best is yet to come "keep hope are life" This book do not intend to hurt anyone's feelings but to tell the truth nothing but the truth about the state of the nation so that this nation can move forward and take care of their own. I felt so sad but I will never forget that night. It was that night that I received the couragement to take action to write this book.

But the night of December 30, 2013, changed everything. It was approximately between 7:00 p.m. to 8:00 p.m. when an unknown fellow stopped me as I was walking home and began talking about Nigerian problems and wanted my help to answer some questions on this issue. This encounter was something that pushed me into action to begin this book. The tone of this stranger about Nigerian problems inspired me and reminded that I have a duty to say something and my voice to the debate.

I am not writing as an authority on this issue but just as someone who loves his nation and wishes it well and just to share my opinion and perhaps open up debate on the serious problems facing the nation so everyone can contribute their opinion.

This paper has talked about reforming Nigeria from top to bottom, and if this is not done, the nation will not go anywhere. A nation that swims in oil money but cannot show to Nigerians and the world one single achievement that can be attributed to oil wealth—it is very, very shameful. The nation cannot hope to move to anywhere under the heat of bribery and corruption, fraud, unemployment, bad education, lack of clean water, lack of electricity, lack of roads, lawlessness, and tribalism—in short, the lack of critical infrastructures.

All hands must be on the deck to make sure that reforms will be successful because Nigerians will get a brand new country after it is over. For reforms to be effectively carried out the government should be dissolve and all active and non-active politicians, political appointees, and all top government officials should be retired. A provisional government should be formed to run the government and stay in power for at least for one to two years in order to oversee the reforms.

Only the current president of the nation can remain in power, pending if Nigerians allows him this privilege. A new generation of men and women should be handed over the government and they should be allowed to be actively involved in reforms.

References

http;/www.blackenterprise.com/small-business/African-american-buying-power-projected-tr
Chioma obi/university graduate/job applicant
Chioma ISAA/university student/Nigeria
Ogochukwu/Polytehnic student/Nigeria
Ebele John/university graduate/job applicant
Ogochukwu madu / university graduate/house wife/job applicant
http;//www.fao.org/docrep/x5032e/x5032e08.htm
http;//www.pbs.org/frontlineworld/stories/bribe/2009/04/niger-delta-more-coverage-0n-the
http;//spanishchef.net/spanishchefblog/2011/10/04/Nigeria-100-percent-cassa.

Dear Nigeria, Africa, America, and the world, we are all a global village people. It is time to begin the debate about how to fix Nigeria and Africa. Please join the debate.

See you on Facebook, Twitter, and Instragram.

General Aguiyi Ironsi

General Odimegwu Ojukwu

General Olusegun Obasanjo

General Yakubu Gowon

Major Patrick Chukuma Kaduna Nzeagwu

President Jonathan Goodluck

President Nelson Mandela

General M. Mohammed 1975

President Shehu Shagari 1979-1983

General M Buhari 1983-1985

General I. Babagida 1985-1993

General Abacha 1993-1998

President Musa Umaru Yar'dua 2007-2010

Martin Luther King Jr.

About the Author

Chukwujiekwu Emmanuel Inyaba-Nwazojie [Chuks] was born in Abatete, Umuebo, Nigeria, and is an ordained church Elder. The president of Seven Stars Import/Export Int. New York, New York. A Nigeria-American. He has been involved in studying the issues about Nigeria.

CPSIA information can be obtained at www.ICGtesting.com
Printed in the USA
BVOW08s2159080916

461473BV00001B/18/P